THE KEEPER

WORLD OF THE VISCEREBUS BOOK 1

OZ MARI G.

ACKNOWLEDGMENTS

The Keeper is my attempt at telling a sweet love story set in a fantastical world. It is also my first YA novel. The book contains elements that I truly love. But it would have ended up as boring were it not for the following people.

My eternal gratitude to:

My best friend for life, Maricar J, for the unwavering support and encouragement, for being always open to read a first draft and point out what my stories lacked.

And the rest of the beta readers who gave me objective feedback.

I dedicate this book to:
My son, Joshua, the inspiration for everything I do.
Finally, to my two cats, iO and Laki, who journeyed with me
with little complaint.

PROLOGUE

It has been told that Prometheus, the creator of all creatures on earth, gave life to two types of being in the likeness of the gods.

The first was the humans who he moulded from clay and earth. He gave them fire as a gift. This generosity infuriated Zeus. He bound Prometheus at Mount Caucasus where the latter's punishment was to have his liver eaten every day by a giant eagle, another titan named Aetos. The liver would regrow every night, and the torturous cycle was to be for thirty thousand years.

Prometheus, legend said, created a pair of second beings as his companions during his suffering. They were not just made in the image of the gods, but from its true essence.

Prometheus added a piece of his liver to the soil and rocks he used to fashion the new creatures, thus bestowing them with superhuman strength, speed, slow aging, and super senses. He also gave them the power to shape shift into animals to enable them to hide from Zeus.

However, he was unaware that the saliva of Aetos tainted a

portion of the liver. And his second creation inherited the need to consume viscera.

He called them Viscerebus, or viscera-eaters.

Once Prometheus was free, he bid the Viscerebus to live among humans. Thus, begun the conflict between the two.

The Viscerebus hunted the humans for their viscera, and the humans hunted them back for survival.

For decades, they were locked in a fierce battle for supremacy. The Viscerebus were stronger, faster, and more powerful, but the humans had centuries of head start in population. They outnumbered the Viscerebus, and it shifted the balance of power.

To protect their own, the Viscerebi formed a Tribunal and engineered a system that ensured the survival of their kind.

They set up a process of procuring fresh viscera without the need to kill humans; the distribution of the victus to their kind to stop them from hunting humans; and the campaign to convince the humans that the Viscerebi were creatures of lore.

They perfected the strategy for millennia, and the Viscerebi thrived, hidden in plain sight among human societies all over the world.

Their success hinged on keeping the Veil of Secrecy intact —the hiding of their existence from the humans at all costs.

But like air, secrets could only be contained through insulation. And like all insulation, it would never be permanent.

When two different beings coexist, their imperfections could create either conflict or cohesion.

1 ASWANG, ERDIA AND HUMAN

Veren stood in the middle of the forest. He breathed deep, trying to pick up the scent of the wild boar he heard foraging. The thick foliage overhead filtered the remaining sunlight, making the forest darker but not dark enough to trigger his night vision.

A breeze blew by him. It carried the smell of the trees, the rotting leaves, the decaying fruits on the forest floor, and the musky odour of the boar. He scanned the direction of the scent until he saw movement two hundred meters away. The animal was digging for something by the roots of the banyan trees.

Veren looked around to see if any of his fellow cadets were close to his location. He centred his senses, listening for human voices, and smelling for them. He could not detect any. With his gun slung behind him to keep his hands free, he lowered his centre of gravity and sprinted towards the unsuspecting boar; the wind whizzed past his ears, the wet squish of the leaves on the ground muffling the sound of his feet.

His speed was too much for the boar. It was a mere split second before the animal realised he was coming. It lifted its head from the ground just before it found itself raised by the hind legs. He swung the boar against the tree trunk, crushing its skull with the force of the blow.

He crouched down and inspected his kill.

Oh, damn... I shattered one tusk.

With a sigh, he took out his handgun and shot the dead boar in the head where the tree had done the most damage. It would be hard to explain to his superior the true cause of its death otherwise. It required tremendous strength to shatter a pig's cranium. A gunshot would be the easiest way to avoid questions.

Inherent caution coloured all of his interactions with humans, just as it did with every single one of his kind. By nature, his kind avoid any potential exposure to their existence. There was no need to alarm the humans and create suspicion.

As he walked back to their camp in the woods, the dead boar slung over his shoulder, he encountered some human hunters along the way. He avoided crossing paths with them. It was easy enough, as he could hear them and their heavy treads on the forest floor. He found himself replying to their conversation in his head.

"I think we should hunt close to that military encampment," one human male said to his companions. There were three of them.

"Why? There are no bandits in these woods."

"Yeah, maybe not, but I heard there are Aswangs."

Yes. There is. Me, he thought.

"Well, we have guns."

"I am not sure if guns can kill Aswangs ..."

Sure they can, if you pump enough bullets in us and we bleed to death before our ability to heal and regenerate catches up.

"Well, what do you think those military men carry as weapons? Guns. And I'm sure they don't use silver bullets."

It was funny how humans had melded one tale of legend into another. For most people, their legends were part of old beliefs, stories passed on through generations and told to scare children. Not one of those tales was accurate.

"I can't believe you still believe in Aswangs ... In this day and age, we would have heard of attacks on humans. We all know what they're after."

To hide their existence, and their need for human viscera, the *Tribunal* had perfected a system of securing much-needed organs without having to kill any humans. Veren believed that it was pure genius to operate most of the funeral parlours, morgues, and mortuaries all over the world. It gave Aswangs access to fresh viscera without the humans' knowledge. The process became seamless over centuries of experience.

"Yeah, not to mention that our military would definitely go after them if they attacked humans. They like nothing better but a reason to kill."

Yes, I agree. And it would be catastrophic to our kind.

Thinking about what the *Tribunal* did for him, how they took care of him, never failed to make his heart swell with gratitude, Veren's vow to serve the community that nurtured him remained his driving goal. And his path to that goal was to become an *Iztari*.

Nothing could be nobler than protecting his kind from the peril that surrounded them all within the human communities. It was a necessity to be in proximity to them, as their need for human viscera was critical to their daily survival.

Military academies all over the world were the natural training grounds for people like him who desired to belong to their elite law enforcement. There were always a few of his kind who graduated every year. Several staffs in the Academy were *Aswangs,* including the Commandant, who took care of supplying them with raw human viscera every three days.

"*It's creepy enough in these woods. Stop your horror stories or we'll be too scared to hunt later.*"

The words of the hunters faded into the distance.

As he walked back to rejoin his troop, his thoughts replayed the discussion other *Aswangs* in the Academy were engaged in last night. There was no one in his class to discuss his opinions with. He was the only *Aswang* there, and he was not close with anyone in the lower and upper classes.

Some of his kind favoured surfacing and showing their might and ruling over the humans. In his opinion, to play on the humans' fear of *Aswangs,* scare them into submission, offered limited value. Fear could be a powerful deterrent, but it tended to wane in potency given enough time. History was littered with toppled governments through revolutions orchestrated by terrified people.

The *Viscerebus* might be stronger, faster, and superior to the humans, but at the odds of thirty to one, even their superior traits could not survive an attack, whether in retaliation or fear. Humans had the numbers and weapons to kill them.

They were safer if they remained hidden in plain sight, unnoticed by the humans and thought of only as a relic of a superstitious past.

Humans were less likely to attack an enemy they did not believe to exist.

Manila, same time, same day.

Anza watched her classmates giggle over selfies with the boys they met at the mall during the weekend. They were on their midday break, waiting for the next class to start. The thought of the boys waiting in the parking lot later excited the three girls. They talked about hanging out with them at the Cosy Café located across the street from the main gate of their school.

The tall and slim Elyse, half-Filipino and half-German, led the girls. The other two were attractive and stylish: Rizzi with her mixed Arabian blood, and Summer's half Chinese heritage. All three were popular and fit the mould of archetypal it-girls. But what really made them unique was they were not mean, hurtful, or selfish, as one might assume.

On the surface, Anza fit the group well. She was petite, slim, and had been told multiple times that she was attractive. She preferred to think these girls wanted her in their group because she tried to match their kindness whenever she could, to compensate for every time she rejected their invitation to go out, and not for her looks.

She wanted to be friends with them, but her father and the laws of the *Viscerebus Tribunal* would not allow it.

"Anza, come with us. They will bring their friend with them. He's interested in meeting you," Elyse prodded her. "He's also into music and photography," she added with a smile.

"Interested in me? How does he know about me?" She had been very careful not to get her pictures on any social media.

"I posted our year-end class photos on my Instagram. He saw it and asked Kirk for an introduction to you," Elyse replied casually.

For her classmates, this was commonplace. Nothing to worry about. For her kind, it was always a concern. It was a footprint to be erased, a snapshot of time that could come back to haunt a slow-ageing *Aswang*. It shouldn't have been an issue for her, because she would age just like a normal human, but she grew up trained in the same rules as her family. It became a habit for her.

"I'm not sure ... My dad won't like it." Her usual alibi was a hundred per cent true.

"Well, they're arriving twenty minutes early, so come with us and chat with them," Elyse implored. "You can leave once your father arrives. Please ..."

All three girls begged her to say yes. It would be embarrassing to say no, and the temptation to give in was strong.

"Okay," she said with a nod.

"Great!" Elyse jumped up from her seat and gave her a quick hug.

She must like that Kirk guy a lot for her to be that excited to make me say yes.

As she watched the three girls chat about their weekend activities, a sense of envy pierced her heart. She wanted to join them. Just once. They asked her every time, and she kept saying no. It was a wonder that they hadn't given up on being nice to her.

Maybe being seatmates helped. She sat behind Elyse, and whenever the trio chatted with each other, she was within hearing range. It was convenient and natural for Elyse to include her in the conversation. As Elyse was the leader of the three, Rizzi and Summer accepted and followed her example.

Two hours later, as she put her things away, she debated whether to tell her father about the early class dismissal today. This meant she wouldn't have to talk to the guy, but Elyse interrupted her thoughts.

"Are you nervous, Anza?" Her smile was gentle and concerned.

She nodded. "A little."

"Why? You're very pretty." Elyse sounded surprised as she looked her over from head to foot.

"It's not my looks that worry me," she began, but Rizzi interjected.

"Anza, with your baby-doll looks, just bat those lashes and you'll have the poor guy eating out of your hand." Rizzi giggled at her own statement.

"Or, you can jam with him. We heard he's a sucker for girls who can sing," Summer added.

Elyse and Rizzi smiled in agreement.

Her classmates misunderstood the source of her reluctance. They didn't know that meeting the boy, no matter how much she liked him after, would never lead to anything. It would be a pointless exercise.

And apart from being forbidden to tell them the truth, they would not believe her even if she broke the *Veil of Secrecy*. They would think her crazy if she told them her entire family was *Aswang*.

That afternoon, for forty minutes, she had a sample of the life she would lead if she inhabited her human heritage. The boy, Mark, was good-looking, charming, and endearingly nervous.

The girls flirted with the boys, laughed at jokes, shared some drinks, and assured that they would see each other again during the coming weekends—the simple joys of connecting with people her age. It was fun, enriching ... and in principle, harmless.

She left them reluctantly. She wanted to stay longer. Not so much because of Mark, but she felt greedy for the moments shared with humans. She had seen what her life could be if her parents allowed her to live the life that her humanity could afford her. She didn't have the long life her parents enjoyed, but they didn't seem to realise this.

Her family was due for *Transit* soon. This meant they would move somewhere far away and new. She would have to go to a new school, meet new people, but couldn't make friends with any of them. And that would repeat in another twenty-five years.

Her life with her family was destined to be limited and lonely, with no one but her parents, uncles, aunts, and cousins as contributors to her experience. She would never fulfil her full potential. She could never have her photos published, her songs sung in airwaves, her poetry read. Just like the contents of her social media, it would just be for her own eyes, like a digital diary.

And this grieved her—the premature death of her potential, the wasting of her life.

Manuu Soledad, the head of his household, came home from a meeting with the *Matriarch* and the *Patriarch* of their *Gentem's Tribunal*.

They discussed the logistics of the *Transit* of Manuu's family, which comprised his daughter and wife.

Normally, this would be a simple arrangement if it just involved his immediate family. But his wife's family, whom they had gotten very close to during the past twelve years, wanted to join them. That required a more extensive logistical setup.

One small family moving into a new community would be unnoticed, but three moving to the same place at the same time would attract attention. The local *Tribunal* decided they could all move to Auckland together, provided they would not live in the same community. Their homes would have to be at least four kilometres apart. At least for the first five years.

For the *Viscerebus,* a *Transit* was a normal part of existence. It was a requirement that they go through every twenty to thirty years, to hide their slow-ageing and longevity. The humans would notice, otherwise.

He was glad the rest of the family would *Transit* with them for the sake of his only daughter, Anza. This was to be her first, and it would be difficult for a teenager like her to cut ties from all her human friends and classmates, to leave behind everything connected to her life in the Philippines.

To have someone close to her age, like her cousin Xandrei, who was so fond of her, would make the process easier on his beloved daughter. She had been quiet and withdrawn for the past few months, especially since the day he did not permit her to attend her school fair. He knew then that she was missing the company of young people.

As his car passed along the coastal road, he thought of the house that he bought in Auckland Bay. His Anza would love it. It offered plenty of photo-worthy scenes. His daughter's poetic soul would appreciate the scenery and the view.

At least, Anza would not have to get used to a new name and identity. He kept their current one. Next year, after Anza finished Year 12, they would fly to their new *Gentem*, to start their *Transit*.

The whole of New Zealand was picturesque. No doubt Anza would enjoy taking photos and writing songs in their new home country.

2 AWAY FROM HOME

V eren slung his duffel bag over his shoulder. They had called him to the *Iztari* head office for a quick briefing. He was planning to take his bag home first, but it was no hardship to pass by the office before going home.

They instructed him to go straight to the office of the *Chief Iztari*, which was on the third floor. He walked into his mentor's corner office with a thrill of anticipation.

Edrigu Orzabal was waiting for him, a smile of satisfaction on his face. Edrigu gave him a tight hug and a thump on the back.

"Congratulations, Veren! Papa told me you graduated top of your class," Edrigu said.

"Thank you, Sir! It was the least I can do," he replied.

He couldn't help but to grin back. It flattered him that his achievement pleased his mentor and Don Lorenzo Ibarra, his sponsor. He thought he owed it to them to do well. They were his only family in this world.

"So, how long do you have before they give you your first deployment?" Edrigu asked.

"I don't know, but we have about a month-long break before we report back to camp for more training," he replied.

"Okay. What do you plan to do with your month?"

"Can I spend it here at the office?" He was hopeful Edrigu would say yes.

"You do not have to. You're allowed to take a break, you know," Edrigu said. He got up and walked to the corner of his office, where a small bar was installed. He pulled out two bottles of cold beer and handed him one.

This surprised him. He didn't realise they could drink in the *Iztari* office. He hesitated.

Edrigu chuckled. "It's allowed during special occasions, and today qualifies," he said in a manner of explanation.

"Thank you, Sir." He accepted the beer.

They clinked their bottles together and toasted to his graduation from the Military Academy. They had spent few companionable moments together.

Veren's heart swelled as he gazed at his mentor, and around the room they were in. The entire building felt like home to him since the first time he stepped into the premises sixteen years ago.

"I prefer to spend my summer break here," Veren said after a moment. "I've always wanted to become an *Iztari*. So, if it's okay with you, Sir, I would love to do this."

Edrigu looked at him, his expression paternal. At least Veren would like to think that was how a father would look at a son—indulgent, patient, and caring. His mentor also seemed to read deeper into him than he cared to think about himself, much less reveal to anyone. Only self-discipline stopped him from looking away.

"Don't you want to spend your summer doing carefree things, like being with people your age, partying, meeting young women, getting a girlfriend, and all those sorts of things?" Edrigu asked. "The opportunities to do that once your work begins will be slim."

"No, Sir. I've spent all my life with people my age. I'm not interested in parties, and while I don't mind meeting girls for a laugh or two, I think it would be unfair to any potential girl-friend of mine to be in a relationship with a man like me, who has no plans of getting serious," he said, and he meant it.

"Okay, if that's what you prefer," Edrigu said, then nodded. "I will train you myself. Come here in the morning at eight a.m. For now, go home and rest. You deserve it." His mentor patted him on the shoulder and gave him a shove toward the door.

"Thank you, Sir. I'll see you tomorrow," he said, giving Edrigu an *Iztari* salute. He took his leave, his duffel bag slung over his shoulders once more.

Edrigu watched his protege walk out. It was a pity the boy was too young for his granddaughter, Yuana, and that she was already deeply involved with a human. Otherwise, he would set them up. Veren was the type of man that any grandfather would want their granddaughter to meet. Smart, intelligent, driven, and with his heart in the right place.

And as he was an *Aswang*, everything would be easier for his granddaughter.

One year later.

Anza wasn't looking forward to today's itinerary. Her father and stepmother, the entire extended family, would go on their quarterly holiday to their mountain lodge. It would be a very long drive, and she had nothing to be excited about for when they would get to their destination.

They would leave her alone in the cabin when they all went out, giving vent to their natural inclination to transform and be themselves.

She couldn't take part in the activities they all looked forward to, which were all geared towards a demonstration of supernatural skills that she didn't have: super strength, super speed, super senses, and shape-shifting. She was the only one in their midst, an *Erdia*, a half-Aswang who shared their blood-line, but none of their powers.

The only thing of value she had for her father's kind was that her viscera could power them better than a human's. At times, she fantasised about incidents where they would need her to give them her liver to save their lives.

But the reality was, the scenario would never happen, and if it did, her father would never allow it.

She was her father's princess, and he treated her like one to a fault. Her parents loved her, and that blinded them to the fact that she was not like them. They treated her like a *Viscerebus*, and raised her to follow the laws and the codes of their world, including the *Veil of Secrecy*.

When they went for their *Transit*, they would expect her to go with them. They would have to move to an unfamiliar country where no one knew who they were. It would be a complete severing of connection with any humans from their previous life.

They seemed to have forgotten the fact that she was as human as her late mother and most of the people in her school. She would age like the humans. And eventually, she would look older than her parents, and she would die long before her parents were halfway through their lifetime.

In the meantime, she would live the Viscerebus life. With

no permanent roots, with no longtime friendships or relationships with any non-*Viscerebus*.

She sighed and got into the car beside her Momstie. She leaned back and closed her eyes, the plush leather comforting, the floral scent of the air freshener familiar. Her parents chatted quietly about the *Transit*. That suited her. She was not in the mood for conversation.

It would be a few hours before they arrived at their destination. A convoy of their families' cars followed theirs. Memories of how she felt as she listened to her classmates talk about going to the movies during the weekend, and of their sleepover tonight, were still fresh. The piercing sense of envy and longing hurt. They invited her, but she had to decline. Her father never allowed her to hang out with her human classmates.

She understood her father's reasoning, always followed his dictates, never doubted that he only meant well, and she used to agree with him. She wasn't so sure anymore.

Four hours later, their car entered the gated compound of their mountain lodge. A thick growth of trees surrounded the property like a wall closing in. The sounds of the forest—the crickets, the birds, the wind that rustled the leaves—were unusually loud. Anza found the familiar fragrance of the wilderness cloying. Everything about it made her uncomfortable. It highlighted the feeling that she didn't want to be here.

Her room in the lodge was unchanged. The caretakers had cleaned it, as expected. The bed and the linens were fresh. They had aired it, for it did not have the musty smell of a room long unused. They would have done all this within a day. Their *Erdia* caretakers lived in the lodge year-round and went on holiday during their visits, leaving them to their privacy whenever they'd come. It was a neat arrangement her family preferred.

With a deep sigh, she looked around her room, her sight landing on her bag. She couldn't be bothered to unpack, so she left it alone. There was nothing much in it, anyway, just the essentials for a three-day break.

She could hear the cacophony of her family outside. They were all in high spirits. Her step-uncle's booming voice dominated as he said something funny. A chorus of laughter followed it. Momstie would be in the kitchen now, supervising the supplies they brought for the weekend - the food, the wine, and everything they would need to spend a memorable family event.

Like before. Like always.

An unwelcome knock pounded on her door. She trudged towards it. It was her cousin, or more correctly, her step-cousin, Xandrei.

"Anz, we'll set up the barbecue outside. Would you like to join us?" The smile on his face was wide and cajoling.

She nodded and followed him out to the verandah.

Xandrei looked down at her, one arm rested against the door as he regarded her. Despite the two-year gap between them and the difference in interests, they were close. Or, as close as she allowed herself to be with him. Xandrei was always attentive to her. He had a depth to him that most people would never know. They bonded over their common love for poetry, which seemed incongruous as Xandrei looked every bit the jock.

And they were both unhappy with their *Viscerebus* trait. In her case, the lack of it. For Xandrei, he found his inability to use his full strength and speed in the sports that he loved, frustrating. There was nothing he could do, because it would violate the *Veil of Secrecy* if he did.

Xandrei compared it to fighting one-handed: it was fun in the beginning, but it became less and less so. Their shared exasperation on this impediment was another reason they had gotten closer in the last five years.

The grill sat on the uncovered portion of the long verandah that wrapped around the lodge. Its position allowed the smoke to waft out into the air once they started cooking. Beside it was a small table laden with raw steaks, marinated chicken breasts and drumsticks, prawns on skewers, corn on the cobs, pineapples, plantains, and pre-baked potatoes wrapped in foil, all ready for the grilling.

Xandrei fired up the grill, while Anza hung back and waited for it to heat. She could see his surreptitious glances. He seemed to sense her disquiet, but he would not ask her directly. He would wait for her to open up. That was Xandrei's way.

He may have to wait for a long time, though, because she didn't know what was wrong with herself, or the source of her unhappiness and dissatisfaction. Her heart was heavy with a combination of grief and anger, a sense of injustice that grew bigger every day.

She was like a keg of gunpowder awaiting contact with a lit fuse that was crawling ever closer.

Anza watched as her cousins horsed around in the gated backyard of their lodge. The ancient trees that surrounded the area seemed bigger and lusher. It added security to the walls that fenced their property. Laughter came louder as the older ones teased the younger ones to the point of annoyance. Immature tempers flared and her younger cousins shifted into their *Animus* out of frustration.

Her fourteen-year-old cousin, a rascal named Caleb, had

been making fun of his sister's crush with Caleb's human friend. The twelve-year-old got so fed up with the antics of her older brother that she, Shelagh, transformed into a hyena. She snarled, growled, and snapped at her older brother. The elders laughed it off. However, their father intervened when Shelagh clamped her jaws on Caleb's calf muscle. He cried out in pain, unable to shake her off.

"Enough, Caleb! Shelagh, stop! You're drawing blood!"

Her uncle's stern voice arrested Shelagh's fury. She let go of her brother's leg and shifted back into her human form. She was teary-eyed out of wrath and frustration. Her brother's blood rimmed her lips.

Caleb glared at his sister. His hand pressed against the bleeding calf muscle that was almost torn off. The bite looked deep, but it would take less than an hour to heal. Her uncle gave Caleb a handkerchief to bind the wound. Shelagh stood with a sullen pout over her brother as she wiped her mouth on the neckline of her pink T-shirt dress and left a streak of a bloodstain on it. Her mother shrieked in exasperation. Blood was hard to remove from cotton fabric.

It's funny that what this household considers commonplace is probably horrific to a human.

Tomorrow, her family would venture into the woods, then shape-shift into a land-based predatory animal to hunt or merely to run around. And by habit, they would leave her alone in the house. It was like being the permanent designated driver when your family and friends went out to get wasted. She was the only one sober, and not by choice.

In the past, she didn't mind. The solitude afforded her time to write songs or poetry, read a book, or take photos. This time, the prospect of being left behind was distressing. She felt... excluded.

She didn't realise the pasted smile on her face had faltered and that she was fidgeting, until Xandrei nudged her side with his elbow.

"Should I hunt him down, Anza?" Xandrei asked, his expression calm. But his eyes bored into hers.

"Who?" She looked up at him, startled.

"Whoever it was who put such a grim frown on your face," he said. Xandrei touched her forehead and stroked the lines away.

"No one did this to me. I was just ... preoccupied."

She walked away and sat in one of the six rattan chairs that lined the verandah. She didn't want to talk about her restlessness, but Xandrei followed and sat beside her.

"Something is bothering you. And if I would hazard a guess, it's your 'otherness,' as you call it. You're back to thinking you're out of place, again," he said, his eyes on her intently.

The truth in his words stabbed at her heart. He read her right. Her discontent had bubbled over the surface. The desire to understand became overwhelming. "How does it feel, Xandrei?"

"Feel what?" Xandrei looked at her, a frown on his forehead.

"To shape-shift. But more to the point, why do you want to?"

It took Xandrei a long moment to respond. His eyes narrowed as he examined his own thoughts. "It's hard to articulate, Anz, but it's like a growing constriction. At first, you hardly notice it, but as the days go, you become uncomfortably trapped, until it becomes a driving need. So, when opportunities to let loose are available, we view it with full enthusiasm."

"Like removing your socks at the end of a long, hot day?" Her lame attempt at analogy made him laugh.

"Yes, actually." Xandrei was still laughing and shaking his head, "It's a very precise analogy, if I may say so."

In a strange way, she could relate to what he described. It was how she felt exactly—trapped. And she wanted to be free. Being unable to do so was driving her to the point of rebellion. Xandrei could remove his proverbial socks, while she could not.

"So, what's bothering you, Anza?" Xandrei's question was serious this time.

"I'm just tired, Xandrei." She avoided his gaze and picked on the loose rattan weave on the chair instead.

"Tired of being the only *Erdia* in a family of Aswangs?"

"I guess ..." It was the closest to admission she could give to him.

To reveal more might give him an idea of what had been brewing in her mind for months now. She wasn't ready to have anyone find out about it, as her plans had not crystallised yet.

Her reticence should have made it clear to Xandrei she was not ready to discuss what was in her heart, but he continued to stare at her with watchful intensity. Her cousin was worried. She patted his hand in reassurance, got up, and went inside to help her stepmother in the kitchen. She needed to go somewhere in which she wouldn't be the discussion or the focus of intense scrutiny.

Her Momstie was preparing the family's *sustenance* for tonight. It was a raw human liver. Her father kept her stepmother company and was gazing at her with soft, loving eyes. She took a seat beside her father, and together they watched Momstie portion the liver in neat, even slices.

Everyone would have a slice, except her. She had seen her parents and her extended family eat raw human viscera countless times, and she was used to the scene. It never bothered her before, but now, her 'otherness' intensified.

She absentmindedly picked up a napkin, twisted it into a thin strip, and fed it into the flame of the lighted cinnamon candle. The napkin burned in slow degrees; its cinnamon scent took on a burnt smell. The rising smoke mesmerised her and took her out of her own mind. It calmed the chaos in her. The curling smoke unravelled into nothingness. She wished the path to her decision would solidify in contrast.

On impulse, her stepmother's soft hands reached out and stopped her. Momstie never liked this habit. She considered it a nervous tick. Her father didn't mind it. He looked at it as a self-soothing habit. Her dad intuitively connected her tendency to set little things alight when she needed to sort out something in her mind.

With a sigh, she dropped the half-burned material at the base of the candle holder.

"Are you okay, Anza?" Her father's gaze was intent. "You're kindling again."

She nodded and said, "I'm okay, Dad. Just bored." She smiled at them both. She didn't want them to probe. Her stepmother had always associated smiles with a positive frame of mind. Hopefully, her Momstie could influence her father. But even she seemed unconvinced.

The voices of their family floated into the kitchen. Everyone was back and had congregated in the living room. It was *sustenance* time. Her Momstie walked off with the bowl of the human liver to where the family waited.

Her father kept looking at her, assessing her. He was wavering between asking her and waiting for her to open up to him. Half of her wanted him to press her, but her other half knew that his response would remain the same. He would, with a gentle and firm voice, tell her she was too young to know her own mind.

Her stepmother popped her head in through the door a moment later. "Anza, the ice delivery guy is coming tomorrow morning. Can you handle it while we're away?" It broke the tension in the air.

"Yes, Momstie," she replied, her tone cheerful.

She didn't mind the errand. It was something to do in a day full of nothing.

That night, in one corner of the living room, the male adults were playing cards while the females were engaged in gossip in the kitchen. The younger ones busied themselves with a board game in the breakfast lounge with more passion than could be expected from the game. Her teenage cousins were, like her, occupied with their gadgets.

Her rambunctious Uncle Heydar, a burly man whose clean-cut look was a complete opposite to his personality, went around the room singing in a deep baritone. The lyrics annoyed the women, but it entertained the young ones.

Her family filled the house with chatter, laughter, and activities. They kept each other entertained with their own antics and stories. Her family was content being themselves. They were complete.

It was beyond her to pretend to be upbeat. She kept to herself, with her headphones on. Music floated in her ears and drowned the hum of noise surrounding her. It helped as everyone was in full volume.

She sat at the corner chair and put up a pretence of chatting with her friends on the phone, looking at social media posts, scrolling past photos and articles, and watching videos. She was the picture of engrossed.

In reality, she was drowning in misery.

"You need not feel like an outsider, Anz. Don't set yourself apart. Choose to belong," Xandrei murmured on her forehead as he dropped an affectionate kiss on it. He left her to her own company and proceeded to his room.

His words made her sit up. It drove the clouds of melancholy from her mind. It sparked an idea of how she could end her inner turmoil.

Choose to belong. Of course!

I have always had a choice, but I never thought about taking the step to claim it.

And I might just have the perfect opportunity tomorrow.

Then, she took in her first freeing breath in months.

Early the following day, the sun was just rising, but their kitchen was already abuzz with activities. Every single one of her family members was preparing for their day out. They would spend the better part of it running in the woods in their *Animus,* hunting for deer, wild boar, or whatever took their fancy.

She would have preferred to stay in bed, to pretend that she was still asleep, so she wouldn't have to see them off. She didn't want to be discouraged from her plan. A knock on her door forced her to get up, to open it and engage with whoever was outside.

It was Xandrei.

"Your mom is calling for you. I think she wants to leave a few instructions."

She knew he didn't miss the signs that she barely slept, but was wise enough to keep his opinion to himself. Her cousin was the soul of diplomacy and tact.

She followed him out to the living room. Everyone was waiting and raring to go. Each one wore a tracksuit and a snapped-on bag strapped diagonally around one shoulder. The bag would keep their clothes and shoes while they were in their animal form, so it would be within easy reach when they'd return to their human forms.

"Anza, the payment for the ice is on the kitchen table. Have them put the twelve bags of ice cubes in the big freezer and the big block in the smaller one," her stepmother said.

"Yes, Momstie," she said.

Her heart had been picking up its beat as the seconds bled away. A plan had crystallised in her head last night, and being left alone was crucial to its execution. She noticed Xandrei had hung back. He didn't seem ready to leave like the rest. He could ruin her plan or remove her time advantage if he stayed.

"Are you not running out with everyone?" she asked.

"Are you okay being alone here, Anza?" He ignored her question, a frown on his face. "I don't want to leave you here by yourself."

"Oh, don't be silly," she said. She pushed him toward the rest. "I'll be fine." She added a lilt in her tone to reassure him.

"No, truly, Anz. I don't mind staying in today," he said.

He stared at her, trying to assess her sincerity. But she heard the reluctance in his voice. Xandrei loved running in the woods in his *Animus* since he never got to do it in the city.

"No, I won't let you pass up this chance to unleash your *Animus*. Don't worry. I'm okay," she insisted.

"Are you sure?" Xandrei's uncertainty was fading.

"Yes," she said, her tone emphatic. "I'll lock up behind you, so I'll be safe. Find me some wild guavas and we're even." She offered him her most reassuring smile. "Go and take off the proverbial socks."

He grinned at the quip, a touch of relief on his face. He dropped a kiss on her forehead, snapped on his own leather bag under his right arm and around his left shoulder, then headed out after the others.

Soon, everyone ran full tilt to the woods. They disappeared behind the thick cover of trees, their shouts of goodbye fading. She rushed to Xandrei's room to get his backpack. She would borrow it without his permission, as it was much better for travelling than her own. It would keep her hands free.

She found it on the chair by the bed, opened but still full. Her cousin, like herself, didn't bother to unpack. She dumped his stuff into a drawer in his wardrobe and slid it shut. A quick search of the many pockets of the bag ensured that she had taken out everything that belonged to him.

She took the backpack into her room and loaded the contents of her own bag into it: extra jeans, two t-shirts, a bath and face towel, toiletries. As an afterthought, she took one of Xandrei's t-shirts from his wardrobe. She would use that as her nightclothes, as she didn't bring her own during this trip. She was in a hurry to finish this before the iceman arrived. With house keys in hand, she took the backpack to the kitchen to wait for the ice delivery.

She had enough time to write her parents two notes. The longer one explained her plan. That should lessen their worry. But she placed it in her father's wallet, where he wouldn't find it as soon as they had returned.

She needed as much time as she could get to cover more distance before they looked for her. Her second, shorter note was a decoy—it said she went to the nearby creek to take some photos. This one she left on the kitchen table, propped against the coffee maker.

She had just finished having breakfast when she heard the approaching truck. Her heart pounded like a giant woodpecker. She stuffed the two water bottles and the sandwiches she packed into a plastic container into her bag.

Ten minutes later, the ice was loaded and stored in the freezer. She paid the men and asked them for a ride to the city.

She told them she needed to buy something, and the old driver obliged. When asked how she was going to come back, she told them her father was going to pick her up.

With the house locked up and a last look around, she hurried out and got into the front with the driver and his assistant for a ride to the city. She wanted to cry, but held herself in check. She had chosen her path, and she needed to follow it. This was where she belonged—with the humans.

And she needed to learn to live as they do.

───────

It surprised Veren when he picked up his phone to find it was Edrigu calling him. He just got home from the *Iztari* office. There must have been something he had forgotten to do.

"Hello, Sir?"

"Veren, can you come back to the office? I have a case for you." Edrigu's voice was even, but there was a sense of urgency in it.

"Yes, Sir. I'll be there in twenty minutes," he replied. He grabbed the backpack he had dropped on his bed just a minute ago.

Sixteen minutes later, he walked back into Edrigu's office. He was on a video call with a worried-looking gentleman.

"Take a seat, Veren," Edrigu said, then turned back to the gentleman on the screen. "Manuu, this is Veren. I think he is the perfect person to find your daughter. As we agreed, we will have more success in getting to her and convincing her to come back home if she doesn't feel threatened by the *Iztaris*."

The man on the screen looked at him closely. He seemed unconvinced. "He looks so young, Drig."

"Veren is twenty-three, well-trained, capable, and he has my complete trust, Manuu. The office will use both approaches so we can recover her in the quickest time possible. But I think Veren will be more successful at this," Edrigu said. "I will send a second team to cover other areas."

Edrigu's trust and open endorsement warmed his heart. But Veren kept his face impassive, his posture erect. He listened and kept all questions to himself. He wanted to receive the full instruction from his mentor before he asked them.

"Okay, I trust your judgment. You know best how to do this," Manuu said, his fatherly concern palpable. "But please hurry, Drig. She's only sixteen and an *Erdia*. She cannot protect herself."

"Don't worry, Manuu. We will get her back. She cannot have gotten that far. Now, send me a copy of her letter to you," Edrigu said. The man nodded and hung up.

Edrigu turned to him. "As you heard, I'm assigning you to this case. Manuu is a good friend of my father-in-law, and his daughter, an *Erdia*, ran away. We need to find her ASAP."

Veren nodded. "She ran away with her boyfriend?" he asked. Such cases were common.

Edrigu shook his head. "No, Manuu does not think so. According to him, Anza has been despondent for the past few months. She didn't seem to want to go in *Transit*. Her cousin said that she was feeling like she doesn't belong with them. She is the only *Erdia* in their closely knit family." Edrigu pushed a copy of the printed picture of the missing girl to him.

He picked up the photo and inspected her image. She was pretty. Long black hair, enormous eyes, innocent-looking face. Almost no makeup. Slim and petite. Around five foot three, at most. She looked younger than her sixteen years suggested.

Could this be an old photo?

She might look different now. Most sixteen year-olds he had met looked far older than their age because of how they dressed and all the makeup they would wear.

28

"Is the picture recent, Sir?"

"Yes, that was taken a month ago, on her sixteenth birthday," Edrigu replied. He printed the attachment that he'd just received from the email. It was the letter from the runaway girl to her father.

Edrigu read it aloud.

"Dear Daddy, please do not be angry. Do not worry. I went to live with the humankind where I belong. I love you and Momstie with all my heart, but I am not like you and the rest of the family. Time will separate us anyway since I do not have your long lives. Let me establish a root here this early. Allow me to find a family that will be like me, mortal and human, while I have the time to do so. This is not forever. When you leave for your Transit, keep our post office box open. Send me a letter there so I know where I can get in touch with you. I will write to you to let you know how I am doing, that I am well. I love you and you will always be in my heart, Anza."

The antics of the runaway girl annoyed Veren. It was too bratty of her to leave her family on a whim, just because she was feeling insecure about being an *Erdia*.

To make her parents worry like that was just petty and inconsiderate. This girl did not know how it was to be an orphan, to be at the mercy of other people's generosity and kindness. She had no idea what it meant to be truly alone.

"How can she be the only *Erdia* in her family, Sir? Her mother should be like her, at least, right?" he asked.

Edrigu shook his head. "No. Her biological mother was human and died of complications during childbirth. She was referring to her stepmother, an *Aswang* who married her father when she was three."

"Okay. So, what do you want me to do, Sir? From what I understood, you want me to find her. Why me and not the *Iztaris*?"

He wanted to get the full picture, the objectives for this case, and what Edrigu expected him to achieve.

"The simple aim is to find her and bring her back. I believe she could relate to you better than my other *Iztaris* because Anza is closer to your age. We don't know for how long she has planned this. Her father said she's smart and organised, just a tad emotional. No doubt because she's still a teenager," Edrigu speculated. "So, if she had planned this well, she would be harder to find. She would factor in our presence and the possibility that the *Iztaris* will try to recover her. She might have prepared for that." His brows knitted in concentration.

"So, does it mean that when I find her, I must bring her back without telling her the *Iztari* office sent me?" he asked.

Edrigu smiled. "Without telling her that an *Iztari* found her."

His eyes widened with disbelief in what he heard, "*Iztari?* Am I one now?"

Edrigu's smile widened. "Yes, this is your first official case. You are the youngest *Iztari* in the history of this office."

"And if I don't find her? If I fail to bring her back?" He still couldn't believe it.

"Don't say that. And you won't fail. But even if you do, the outcome will not affect your appointment. When you return, you will begin your Iztari fight training. Welcome to the team." Edrigu held out his hand to shake his.

He clasped it tight. In his gratitude, he shook his mentor's hand with vigour. "I will not let you down, Sir," he said, too excited to say more.

Edrigu laughed. "I'm convinced you won't. So off you go. I gave you access to her file. Learn about her tonight, and you will be off to the area where she was last seen—Tuguegarao City. From there, you will figure out where she could have gone to hide."

"Okay, thank you, Sir. I appreciate this opportunity," he said, giddy and fired up at the same time.

With a quick *Iztari* salute, Veren left the office. He had to stop himself from jumping with joy. His blood was afire with excitement, ready to begin the preparation for the case.

He was confident he would find her and bring her home no matter what. Even if he had to sedate her the whole way back.

3 A NEW MISSION

Veren sat in a local coffee shop in Tuguegarao City. He didn't expect it to be so dense with low-rise buildings and people. The streets were typical of small cities: tight four lanes of concrete with almost no sidewalk. Old homes made of wood and stone and semi-new buildings made of glass and cement stood side by side along the road. Cars, jeepneys, and tricycles roamed the roads in a noisy parade, but there wasn't much traffic. Their pace was slow, but steady.

He was waiting for the man who delivered ice to the household of Anza Soledad, the last person who saw her. According to Manuu Soledad, the man gave Anza a ride to the city and dropped her off across the street. Then, he drove away. Still, Veren wanted to interview the man himself to see if he could pick more clues that the Soledads missed.

While he waited, he reviewed the digital file of his subject, everything about her on record and whatever else he had learned from her family. Aetheranza Soledad, or Anza, as her parents Manuu and Leire Soledad called her.

Interesting name.

If there was one dead giveaway for an *Aswang* parentage, it was their name. Their kind had a penchant for very ancient and unusual names for their children.

He was glad that his target had social media. As an *Erdia,* she had an advantage over *Aswangs* like himself—their Tribunal allowed her the leeway to create a social media account, for as long as there was no exposure of her *Aswang* relatives in it.

The photos of her showed a well-dressed young girl, fashionable even. Her social media was as extensive as any average human teenager. She filled it with pictures of her travels, the books she read, movies she watched, places she dined in. There were brief clips of her singing songs she wrote herself. Her voice was sweet and clear, almost angelic.

The contents of her pages were engaging. She could easily be a popular influencer, if not for one specific thing—she did not have followers. It was like she designed her social media to be a journal; it was private and exclusive to herself. A record of the moments of her life, to be reviewed later in old age.

That struck a chord in him.

Her family said that she was good at school. She was passionate and strong-willed, but otherwise a dutiful daughter. Her father and stepmother gave him differing opinions on her personality.

According to Manuu Soledad, she was a book-loving, introverted girl. Reserved, observant, and content to be by herself.

Her stepmother disagreed—she claimed Anza loved poetry and music, but she craved affection and social interaction. It would seem her stepmother was correct in that aspect.

He thought about the other information provided to him by her family. He knew she carried little, as she came to the lodge with a small bag. And she borrowed her cousin's backpack. This meant that more than likely, she saw an opportunity to leave, that this was impulsive rather than a pre-planned action.

"Mr. Albareda?"

An older man stood by his table. He looked to be in his mid-fifties, with sun-browned skin and thinning hair. He smelled of the sun, sweat and a tinge of coolant. The man had one arm darker than the other, which told Veren that he drove with the said arm propped on the window of the truck.

He nodded in acknowledgement, "Mang Andong?"

Veren stood up and offered his hand to the man, who shook it after a moment of hesitation. The older man's grip was limp and weak; the hand was dusty.

Mang Andong took the seat he offered, and after their order of coffee arrived, the man asked him, "What can I do for you, Mr. Albareda?"

"Our family asked me to look for my cousin, Anza. I believe you gave her a ride from the lodge and dropped her off here?"

This was the practised spiel he agreed on with the Soledad family.

"Yes. I told them that already," the man said with a nod.

As Manuu Soledad told him, Mang Andong seemed very open and cooperative. Veren's tablet was open and ready to note what Mang Andong would say. He was also taping their conversation, so he could review it later.

"Yes, Sir. My uncle told me you did. Did you notice anything about her? Did she say or ask you about anything during the ride? Was she carrying anything with her?"

Mang Andong was quiet for a moment as he dredged his memory.

"No, I don't think so. She just said thank you when she first got into the truck and thank you when she got off. She saw this coffee shop and asked to be let off here. That's where I dropped her off." He pointed to the open space across from the coffee shop.

Veren looked out at it. There was nothing of note on that side of the road.

"Did she ask to be dropped off at this coffee shop in particular?"

"No ... not really ... I guess I just assumed. It was early morning, and this coffee shop is popular with the local teenagers. I thought she needed breakfast," he said.

Veren looked around and realised that Mang Andong was right. It was now getting filled with young people, coming in small groups of two or three.

"Did you see her go into the shop?" He wanted that clarified.

"No, but I looked at the side mirror and I saw her cross the street. That was it." The man took a careful sip from his styrofoam cup. "I hope you find her. She's so young," Mang Andong said, his face serious, his tone touched with concern.

"I hope so, too, Sir," he said. "Thank you for your help." He shook the kind gentleman's hand for the second time.

When Mang Andong left, Veren got out to the front of the coffee shop and surveyed the area. There was nothing of note until he realised there was a small travel agency three doors away. It was closed at the moment, but it could be worth looking into later.

When he got back to his table, the manager of the coffee shop hovered near it. He had requested to speak to her earlier, but she was not in yet. She was here now.

"My staff said that you were looking for me?"

A human female in her mid-thirties asked this with a slight frown on her face. She smelled of cinnamon, baked bread, and the coffee powder that dusted her right-hand sleeve. She must have ground some coffee beans and transferred them to a jar.

He nodded.

"Yes, I just want to ask some questions about my missing cousin. We believe she may have stopped here two days ago." He handed her the picture of Anza. "She looks like this."

The woman looked at it, trying to recall. "I'm sure I didn't encounter her—I'm good with faces. Approximately, what time do you think she might have come in here?"

"Around eight to eight-thirty a.m."

"My assistant may have come across her. I was on the afternoon shift two days ago. He won't be here until after lunch, around one p.m. You can come back to ask him later," she suggested.

"Thank you, I'll do that," he said, nodding.

"Anything else I can help you with?" she asked. Her unremarkable facial features changed into something pleasant as she smiled.

"Ah ... What time does that travel agency next door open?" he asked.

"Oh, you mean the Travel Bug? That office has been closed for a few months now. They transferred near the City Hall," she replied.

"Oh, okay. I'll check them out." He stowed his work tablet into his backpack, zipped it close, then slung it over his shoulder. "I will return here at one-thirty p.m., if that's okay."

"Sure. See you later," the manager said.

He left the shop and walked to the nearby Travel Bug to examine it. Faded stickers of airline logos and posters of tourist sites and destinations covered the dirty glass doors. There was a sign on the wall that said, 'WE TRANSFERRED TO OUR NEW LOCATION.' A map of the new address was included. He snapped a photo. This was where he was going next.

If Anza came here, she must have looked at the window display. He noticed the most prominently displayed picture was Batanes island, and remembered the destination shots she had posted on her social media.

The island might appeal to her poetic soul.

He had a gut feel about it, and was convinced she went to Batanes, but his mind told him not to jump to the conclusion. He didn't know her very well. Batanes Island might not meet her standards. She grew up in comfort and luxury. The island's rustic reputation might have dissuaded her.

He walked to the travel agency's new location, a mere four blocks away from their old one. Their new office was cramped, with mismatched tables and chairs, set back-to-back with each other. Two old metal file cabinets were set against the far wall. It had the usual chaos of phone ringing, a pair of dusty computers, and plastic inbox trays piled high with various documents. Though the staff accommodated his questions, the interview yielded nothing. Anza didn't go there at all.

He spent that morning walking around the area. He noted the structures he passed by: small stores, and some middle-sized houses in between commercial spaces. Anza would not take up residence here, he thought. It was too close to their mountain lodge. If she had wanted to disappear as she stated in her letter, she would go somewhere else. The city would only be her jump-off point.

He asked some locals who he encountered along the street where the bus station was, and they directed him to it. It was another couple of blocks away. He found a big, covered area with greasy, gravelled ground. The air stank of petrol and burnt tires. There were about ten buses parked. He noted the various destinations the bus company covered, and his spirit sank a little.

If she took one of the buses from here, she could be anywhere.

He interviewed the ticket officer, a man in a grimy brown shirt and a paunch. While the man was sure he had never encountered Anza, he was kind enough to call in the bus drivers and their assistants to ask if they saw her on any of their trips. No one had seen her. Of course, it was possible they just didn't remember seeing her.

"Maybe she went to Batanes," the ticket officer said out of the blue.

It made Veren's heart jump. "How do you get to the island from here?" he asked.

"You fly. There's no other way." The ticket officer shrugged. The man turned to the line of ticket buyers that accumulated behind him during their discussion.

Veren walked back to the coffee shop to have lunch and waited for the assistant manager. His thoughts were full of the possibilities of Batanes. He would need consent from Anza's parents to secure her flight information if she flew there. The airlines would never give it to him otherwise.

The coffee shop was full of diners when he arrived. A smiling manager welcomed him as he entered.

"You're back. My assistant will be here in half an hour. Will you have lunch while you wait?" she asked, her smile turned expectant.

"Yeah, that's the plan," he said, and smiled back in response.

"Good. Thank you for contributing to the local economy."

She looked around for a second and found him a seat in the shop's corner. He ordered coffee and meat pie.

Forty-five minutes later, the manager brought the assistant over and introduced him. He was a younger man, though older than him, with a pleasant, round face.

"Mr. Albareda, this is my assistant. Clyde, Mr. Albareda here wanted to talk to you about his cousin. He's looking for her and was wondering if she came here during your shift two days ago," she said in a manner of introduction.

He shook the man's hand, and they both sat down together at his table. He showed Clyde the picture of Anza, who looked at it, his brows knitted together.

"I think she came in here and bought a drink," he drawled.

The information raised his hopes.

"Did she say anything? Mention anything at all?" he asked, mentally crossing his fingers.

"Not to me. But she spoke to the guard briefly before she left. I think she was asking for direction," Clyde said.

"Can I speak to your guard?" Impatience rode him.

"Sure, let me call him." Clyde raised his hand and beckoned the guard over, who approached them.

"Yes, Sir?" The guard inclined his head to Clyde.

"Manong, do you remember this girl?" Clyde showed him the picture of Anza. "She was here two days ago."

"Oh yes, I remember." The guard's face brightened in recognition. "She asked me where the airport was, and how to get there," he replied.

Veren's heart jumped in excitement at his words. That was a solid lead.

"Did she say anything else, Sir?" he asked, wanting to make sure.

The guard shook his head.

With a thank you, he left them and hurried to the airport. He knew where it was. Half an hour later, he was in a queue at the ticketing office. As expected, the airline staff would not divulge details of Anza's flight. He expected it, but it was still frustrating. He would lose some time to secure the required affidavit.

With one last effort, he tried to get the cooperation of the counter staff. A female human who, he realised, was flirting with him. He gave her his best smile as he pleaded his case. She shook her head regretfully.

"I really can't—it's company policy. Besides, Mr. Albareda, she would have needed a written consent form from an adult to book her flight. She's a minor."

That information made him sit up.

"Is there any other way that she could have gotten a seat without the consent form?" He was so sure in his gut that Anza took this route. She would not travel by bus anywhere.

"Hmm, well, if she booked through a travel agency, then we can only check her in. And the only thing we would require during check-in is her ID," she said.

"Where is the closest travel agency?" he asked her, his own smile conspiratorial. Hers widened.

"There are three in the building next door," she replied. "Try the first one on the left," she added.

He took her hand and clasped it tightly in gratitude. "I will look for you when I check-in," he said.

She looped her hair behind her ear, looking up at him from behind her lashes. For a moment, he was thankful for the genes he inherited from his parents, whoever they were. To be decent-looking had definite benefits.

Veren rushed to the building next door and went to the one the ticket officer hinted at. He got lucky. He encountered the woman who handled Anza's airline reservation and ticket. She confirmed his hunch. Anza flew to Batanes Island that same day. She was lucky to have caught that day's flight by chance.

Veren booked himself for the following day. He was fortunate the low season made it possible for him to secure a seat, as flights to the island were only three times a week. The travel agent said that during peak periods, the seats would be booked to capacity weeks in advance.

With a satisfied sigh, he contacted Anza's father to inform him where he was going. It took him a few minutes to pacify Manuu Soledad and convince him not to fly to Batanes, as they do not know exactly where she was, and she might just bolt again if spooked.

He took a room in an inn close to the airport and to spend the rest of the day researching about the island Anza disappeared to and reviewing her files.

Batanes Island's population was too small to support an Aswang, much less a community. No viable source for *victus*, or fresh human viscera that he needed to stabilise his human form. With his consumption of *sustenance* yesterday, he would have five days to find and bring Anza home before he would need to fly back to the mainland to secure his *victus*.

It was best to focus on his target.

He needed all the information he could find out about Anza. His mission required him to approach her incognito. Her father didn't want her to be returned by force or by guile to the family, he wanted Anza to come home voluntarily. Manuu Soledad was afraid that if forced, she might run away again, never to be found.

She could not know that he was an *Iztari*. Based on what he found out about her, she could be wilful. This meant he needed to be as cunning as he could be to convince this girl to come home on her own accord. Sedating her into unconsciousness was not an option.

It's a pity... That would be easier.

Anza looked around at her rented room. The room was neat, with pastel-coloured walls, floral curtains and bedspread. Everything about it appealed to her, especially the beautiful garden view and the cosy verandah. The breeze that wafted from the open door brought the fragrance of jasmine, which covered the garden below.

She really liked it here. It made her feel safe and at home, but she would have to leave this place to find cheaper accommodation and a job.

When I find a stable job, I will come back to this room and rent it for a day as a reward. Hopefully, it won't take long.

She needed to find a job before she ran out of cash. The money she had withdrawn from the ATM two days ago would not go very far. She would have taken more if there was no maximum limit, and she didn't want to make another withdrawal here, as that would pinpoint her location. Her father would trace her through her credit card and ATM use. Paying in cash was the way to go for her.

She missed her father and stepmother. And she was guilt ridden for ruining their holiday. By now, her parents would be frantic. And for sure, they had already deployed the *Iztaris* after her. Hopefully, she had covered her tracks well enough. She hoped that when they'd find her, she would be settled and have a good job to convince her father that they could leave her behind to live on her own and be independent.

With a heavy heart, she picked up her backpack. Another day of looking for a job. A glance in the mirror startled her, her look still unfamiliar. She had her hair dyed a lighter brown, cut shorter just past her shoulders from its usual waist length. She styled it in a more sophisticated way.

The negative feedback from the jobs she applied to was mostly because of her age. No one wanted to accept her because she looked too young. Today, with her new hairstyle and the full make-up, she looked older. Hopefully, this would also help hide her from the *Iztaris*.

On her itinerary today: quick breakfast first, then an entire day of job hunting.

Four hours later, she was unsuccessful, tired, and demoralised. She didn't have any experience and couldn't provide any references from any of the locals. They gave her pitying looks, advice to go home and focus on her studies, and sent her off. No one wanted to hire a strange girl who looked like she had never done a day's work in her life.

Her footsteps were as leaden as her heart as she sat down on a plastic chair outside a small, local eatery. She was hungry, thirsty, and close to tears. A prepubescent girl approached her with a laminated menu.

"Miss, what would you like to order?" she asked, without glancing at her, her focus on the small pad of paper in her hand, pen poised to write.

Anza took a deep breath to steady her emotions and glanced at the menu. She had scrambled eggs and toast for breakfast, which was not adequate fuel for all the walking she did this morning. She ordered noodles and a boiled egg for protein. She must learn to live and eat simply until she could afford it.

Her food arrived, served hot by the same girl. The server also placed a cold, light brown beverage on the old, Formica-covered table.

"I didn't order this ..." she began. She wanted to keep to her budget, to stretch her cash as far as she could.

"It's free with every order. It's house iced tea." The girl informed her, her tone dispassionate, and then left her to usher in a couple who just arrived.

Anza mumbled her thanks to the girl's departing back. She felt overwhelmed by a stroke of good fortune, and a wave of self-pity followed in its wake. Her chest tightened as she tried to control the expanding pain that bloomed in her heart. Hot tears pricked at the back of her eyes. She breathed deep and tucked into her noodles to stem the desire to cry.

But she couldn't stop the tears from running down her cheeks. She was truly alone, in a situation she made for herself, one she still believed was necessary for her future.

It was hard to chew when her jaw was taut with the effort to keep her sobs in. She was thankful that the noodles, aided by the broth, just slid down her throat. The hot broth warmed her stomach and soothed even her throbbing heart.

It fortified her.

She took a deep, shuddering breath. Crying would not help her situation. She wiped the tears on her face, resolved to continue her search for a job. She forced herself to finish her noodles and the egg. Her appetite left her two spoonfuls ago, but she needed to eat and didn't want to waste food. She had the rest of the afternoon to accomplish her immediate goal. She needed fuel.

With renewed faith in herself, she considered what her new strategy would be. This time she needed to find a reference, and she had an idea who she would approach. A glance in her hand mirror told her she needed to fix her face. Her mascara smudged when she wiped her hand across her eyes, and her tears created tracks on her cheeks. She didn't know how to fix her makeup without her kit.

She got up and proceeded to the ladies' room.

Ten minutes later, fresh-faced and determined, she went back to her inn. She needed her landlord's help. Hopefully, Mrs. Bassig would be generous enough to extend her a helping hand.

Veren wanted something to perk him up. His flight was an unpleasant experience. It was delayed and the voyage itself was bumpy. He was hungry, and he lost time. Anger borne out of frustration tightened his chest, but it was useless to fume about the wasted morning.

He would have to make up lost ground in the afternoon.

The outdoor seating in the coffee shop provided an ambience that suited the area and his need for a calming influence. It reflected the spirit of the island—quaint, cosy, and relaxed. The wide cream and brown awning overhead softened the sun's glare, and the breeze that ruffled his hair was lukewarm.

He sat outside to drink his coffee and was savouring the first sip when he noticed a young woman across the street. He watched her walk to the local eatery, her shoulders slumped, head bowed—her posture telegraphed defeat and misery.

Seeing a familiar emotion in another person called out to some part of him.

He averted his eyes to shake away the sentiment that resurfaced in him, because he had no time to feel sorry for a stranger. He had a job to do, and he needed to focus. To find his target might take more than the time he had on his hands, and he did not want to fail.

But he found himself drawn to the woman. He could see how upset she was. Her shoulder-length hair could not hide the tautness in her jaw as she fought against her pain, or the movement in her throat as she swallowed down her emotions. Tears glistened on her cheeks as she hunched over her bowl of noodles. He noticed the struggle in her as she tried to control her shoulders from shaking.

And his heart contracted in sympathy.

Then her spine straightened, her chest expanded as she drew a breath. Fascinated, he saw her pull herself together and wipe the tears with the back of her hand like a child. He heard the deep indrawn breath as she fortified her courage. And he could not help but admire the way she recovered so fast from whatever devastation she had suffered earlier. She looked less like a child and more a woman at that moment.

He wished, for an instant, that his quarry, Anza Soledad, was as evocative as this unknown woman across the street.

She continued eating with the grim determination of a soldier who decided to plough into battle. Her fighting spirit showed clearly in the straightened line of her back and the stubborn jut of her jaw. Then she stood up and went inside the local eatery, presumably to fix herself. He waited with anticipation for her to come out again. For a second, he thought he lost her through a backdoor and was disappointed, but when she came out, his heart stopped.

Her face wiped clean, her hair tied in a ponytail, he recognised who his crying lady was—Anza Soledad.

His target.

I found her.

A thrill of satisfaction ran through him.

Veren jumped up and followed her as she crossed the street. He kept a decent distance between them, making sure that she was always within sight.

Her eventual destination was an inn that looked like a renovated ancestral home. She walked into the lobby with purpose and familiarity. She approached the counter. The staff seemed to recognise her, their manner familiar, their smiles welcoming. He saw her sit on the couch. She looked like she was waiting for someone.

He didn't want to book a room until he was sure that she was staying here. He took a brochure, chose a seat close to her, and pretended to peruse the material. Then an idea struck him. He turned to her with a slight smile.

"Miss, are you staying here?" he asked. "How are the rooms?" He kept his tone and facial expression neutral and mild, so as not to alarm her.

"It's nice here. Clean, secure, and the staff are friendly," she replied, her expression polite, but not inviting any further exchange. Natural restraint ruled her interaction with strangers.

Her parents trained her well. She didn't confirm if she was staying here.

A buxom older woman, her grey-tinged hair set in a loose bun, came out from behind the reception counter and drew Anza's attention. The front office staff pointed at Anza. The woman smiled from a distance and beckoned Anza over.

Anza stood up and hastened towards her. He followed on the pretext of inquiring for a room. Their conversation reached his ears clearly.

"Anza, what can I do for you?" The older woman asked, her gaze soft.

"I have a favour to ask, Mrs. Bassig," Anza replied. Her tone was hesitant, almost shy.

The older woman looked surprised, but smiled just the same. She invited Anza into her office. Anza complied and followed Mrs. Bassig to the room behind the reception desk. The door closed on his ability to eavesdrop.

He trusted his instinct and booked himself a room. The only way for the manager to know Anza, and for Anza to have enough confidence to ask for a favour from the older woman, was because she was staying here.

He took his time filling up the registration form. And when he got his key and Anza had not come out yet from the office, he asked the front desk staff for tourist site suggestions. With the tourism brochures in hand, he stood by the counter and made a show of studying them with careful intent.

A few minutes later, Anza came out of the office with a bright smile and sparkling eyes. She looked both relieved and excited. She thanked Mrs. Bassig profusely.

"So, when do you want to start, Anza?" the older woman asked.

"It's up to you, Mrs. Bassig, but I'm ready to start anytime."

"Why don't you check out the place that I recommended to you first? Get yourself settled and then we can start your training on Monday. Iza, the one you will replace, will not be available to train you till then," Mrs. Bassig said.

"Okay, Mrs. Bassig. I'm very grateful. I don't know how to thank you," Anza said. There was a slight tremble in her voice.

"Do your best, Anza—that will be the thank you I want," Mrs. Bassig said, and with an affectionate pat on her shoulder, the older woman left Anza, who stood teary-eyed as if she still could not believe her luck.

"Congratulations!" Veren said in a soft tone, startling her.

"Excuse me?" she asked, blinking her tears away. "It looks like you got the job," he said, pointing back towards the reception area. At her silence, he added, "Sorry, I can't help but overhear. I was checking in."

"Oh ... Yes. I did," she replied. Her earlier relief coloured her voice and tinted her smile.

"Well, I took your recommendation and got a room here. So, thank you," he said.

"You're welcome. How long are you staying?" Her response was automatic, out of politeness rather than from genuine interest.

"I don't know yet." He shrugged. It was the truth.

"Long holiday?" she asked. Her question, this time, carried a tinge of curiosity.

"Yes, maybe," he replied. "How about you?" He wanted to keep his lies to her to a minimum. Perhaps he could pick up some more information about her.

She just gave him a sad, brief smile. A spark of fear and

determination glowed in her eyes. The flash of pride and protectiveness rose in him, and it took him by surprise.

"So, I'll see you around?" she asked, but her tone carried no expectation. She was being polite once again.

"Yes, definitely. Hopefully this afternoon?" He turned on the charm now, his smile friendly and harmless. Now that he found her, she was in his keeping, and would remain under his protection until she returned home.

"This afternoon?" she asked, a slight frown appeared on her brow.

"Yes, I would like to invite you for coffee. For helping me find good accommodation," he said with a deeper smile.

"Ah ... I'm not sure." Her rejection sounded like an automatic reaction. "Um ... I need to check out a place that Mrs. Bassig recommended to me," she said, reluctant and regretful at the same time. Her smile dimmed.

"Can I come with you?" he asked. "I have nothing else to do ..." When she didn't respond, he said, "I would like to explore the area, mingle with the locals, and I don't want to look like a loser by walking alone ...".

She hesitated for a while, regarding him with careful intent. He kept his expression benign and waited for her reply. Finally, she gave him a shy smile and nodded. "Okay."

He couldn't hide his obvious delight at her response. "So, what time are we leaving?"

"I was thinking of doing that now," she said.

"Well then, let's go," he said, and held her elbow.

She threw him a speculative glance. He could see her prudent side warred with her desire to socialise, to connect with another human being. He gave her another reassuring, friendly look, to tip the balance in his favour.

She returned it, and walked towards her destination. He took a relaxed step beside her, pleased with this minor success.

4 CROSSING OF PATHS

Anza was very aware of the man walking beside her. She watched him through her peripheral vision. He was lithe and fit, like an athlete. If she was to guess, he would be a swimmer, based on the width of his shoulders. And he was tall; her head came up to the middle of his chest. His skin had a slight tan, a sign that he enjoyed spending time outdoors. And while he seemed relaxed in his manner, he moved with a certain controlled gait that reminded her of soldiers.

"My name is Veren—Veren Albareda," he said.

He offered his right hand to her. She stopped, looked up at him, then grasped his offered hand. His grip was warm, his hand big enough to envelop both of hers. Manual tasks had roughened his palm.

"I'm Anza," she replied.

Her voice faltered as she took a full look at his face. His eyes were almond-shaped, their colour an odd light brown with amber flecks, framed by straight brows that almost didn't taper at the ends. There was a slight, natural bump on his nose. His lean cheeks and square jaw reminded her of her father. There was nothing remarkable in the individual features of his face, but combined, the result was striking.

It was hard to guess how old he was. He seemed both young and mature, but if she would warrant a guess, he would be in his early twenties.

"Do you have a last name, Anza?" he asked. His lips curved in a crooked smile.

The sight of it made her retract her earlier description of his facial features. His lips were remarkable. They were full, yet masculine. Most of the men in her family had a thin upper lip.

"Sol ... Soledad," she replied. She was uncertain if it was a good idea to tell him her last name. She glanced at him again, gauging her own instinct about him. He looked too young to be an *Iztari*.

"I'm very pleased to meet you, Anza Soledad," he said. He seemed pleased with her response.

"Likewise," she replied.

He covered her hand he still held with the other, and shook it once again. She pulled her hand away—his warm grasp made her fingers tingle. She resumed their walk to mask her nervousness. He fell beside her with effortless grace, shortening his gait to match hers.

"So, are you from this region?" he asked.

She shook her head. "No, I'm from the ... south," she replied. She didn't want to reveal more information about herself.

"South, like Batangas? Or like Cebu?" Veren's eyebrow raised in inquiry.

"Not as far south as Cebu. Closer to Batangas," she replied. She braced herself for more questions, but Veren surprised her by dropping the topic.

"So, where are we going?" he asked instead.

"Ah, it's a bed space place. Mrs. Bassig recommended it," she replied.

"Bed space? You're no longer staying at Mrs. Bassig's?" He seemed alarmed at the thought.

"I can't afford to stay there. My future salary will not be enough to cover my cost of living." It was painful to accept that she was no longer the Anza Soledad who never had to worry about basic survival needs like food and shelter.

Veren touched her elbow, halting her step. He stared at her, as if trying to understand why she needed to work.

"Are you in trouble, Anza?"

His question startled her.

She shook her head. "No," she replied. She didn't know what else to say.

"Okay, but if you are, let me know. I'm your bodyguard, after all," Veren said, his tone light, almost joking, but she could detect an underlying seriousness in his statement.

She didn't know what to think, so she walked on. They found the house exactly where and how it was described by Mrs. Bassig. It was a medium-sized structure, made of stone and wood, old but well maintained, with a colourful garden in front and surrounded by a white wooden fence made of driftwood.

Low, thick bushes with tiny red and white flowers reinforced the fence. There were clucking chickens roaming and pecking around the garden, and a small triangular roof-like structure on the ground with a rooster perched on top of it. The wooden gate was low, with a number 32 painted on it.

The thin, elderly owner named Teresa ushered them into her living room. The windows to the house were all open, the short flowery curtains that swayed with the breeze providing privacy to the residents. The house smelled of fried bananas and ginger tea. Her furniture was made of similar driftwood material, upholstered in green floral fabric.

"Hija, I have no available bed space today. The next available one would be on Tuesday. I can reserve that for you if you want to wait," she said after she set the ginger tea and bananas covered in crispy batter in front of them.

Her heart sank. A week away. That would mean she would have to spend more of her money on her accommodation, something she would rather not do.

Could there be other options?

"Do you know of any other bed spaces here?" At least a temporary one until Tuesday.

"My brother operates one. It's in the next barangay, so it's quite a walk from your workplace. Plus, he accepts male bed-spacers, too, so you might not feel comfortable with that." The elderly woman glanced at Veren beside her; she seemed to gauge what their relationship was.

Veren's gaze was intent on her. His face was impassive, but Anza sensed that he didn't like the idea of her sleeping in proximity with strange men. She didn't like it either. However, the landlady was looking at her expectantly, waiting for her response, and she didn't know what to say.

"Manang Teresa, can you give us the phone number of your brother? And yours as well. Anza needs to think about it," Veren suggested. The old lady nodded and wrote the numbers down on a piece of paper, then handed it to him.

They took their leave and strolled back to their inn. Her mind juggled her options. A week's stay at her current accommodation could cover five months of rent in the bed space place.

Maybe I could stay at the other bed space for a week and then move to Manang Teresa's after?

She was so preoccupied with her own thoughts that she didn't notice when Veren pulled her to a small cafe. At her puzzled look, he pointed at the sign and said, "Coffee, remember? I owe you one."

"Okay." She allowed herself to be pushed gently to a chair.

"What would you like?"

"Mocha or latte," she replied.

He nodded and approached the counter.

Moments later, Veren came back with two lattes. They sipped their respective cups in silence. Out of habit, she pulled out a paper napkin from the holder, twisted it into a thin strip, and fed it into the flame of the lit candle on the table. Calm settled in her as she watched the smoke spiral upwards. With it, the earlier dismay for the situation.

Veren set his cup down. It startled her out of her reverie and made her drop the napkin on the table. She looked up to find his eyes on her.

"Anza. I hope I don't appear a presumptuous prick to you ... Granted, we just met, and I still fall in the category of a stranger, but ..." His statement faded, and an awkward silence followed.

"But?" She wasn't sure what he wanted to say.

"I'm not comfortable with you sleeping in a house where there are strange men. It sounds dangerous," he said, face serious.

She didn't know what to say to that, given that she had the same concern. "It doesn't seem so different from having a room in an Airbnb like Mrs. Bassig's." Her defence to justify the plan was half-hearted.

"It's different. You get your own room in Mrs. Bassig's. In a bed space, you'll end up sharing a room with others. Hopefully, all women, but you might be unlucky enough to bunk in with a man. How will you be able to sleep when you have valuables to guard?"

To hear him say it made her feel worse that she had even considered staying there for a week.

"Veren, an extra week at Mrs. Bassig's is equivalent to five months of rent at Manang Teresa's. I think I can handle a—a week." Her voice faltered at the look of alarm on Veren's face.

After a moment, he said, "I have a suggestion."

"What is it?"

"If I hire you as my tour guide for a week at the cost of what you pay for your current room at Mrs. Bassig's, would you do it?" he asked.

"What? I'm not qualified to be a tour guide ... I'm also a visitor here. I just arrived and I don't know the area at all." She said this weakly—his offer had her heart pounding with hope.

"Okay, as a travel companion then," he suggested.

His offer was perplexing, and his persistence baffled her. "But ... why? Why are you helping me?"

"Why not?" He shrugged. "To travel with friends is always better than travelling alone," he reasoned.

She looked at him, trying to find a reason to say no. His offer was so tempting as a much-needed lifeline.

"But I can't afford the cost of travelling with you. The transportation, the food, the entrance fees ..." The reality of her financial status dampened her hope.

"I'll take care of all that. So, don't worry," Veren said, confidence reassuring.

"It seems... unfair to you. Taking me with you as you go around would double your cost, then add what you would pay me every day. It sounds excessive." She was unwilling to take advantage of him, even if his offer was god-sent.

Veren considered what she said for a moment, thinking.

"Okay then, while we're travelling together, would you consider telling me about you? I'll pay for your stories and that would cover the cost of the travel. Your daily fee will be for the companionship." The matter-of-fact way he explained this made it sound like a fair trade.

"What happens if you tire of my company, or I bore you with my stories?"

"That's a risk I am willing to take ... So, is that a deal?"

There was no reason to decline his offer. It would solve her problem, and she had another week of staying in relative comfort. As much as she wanted to ignore it, he had been pleasant so far, and he intrigued her.

She took a deep breath and decided to trust him. She offered her hand, and they shook on it.

"When do we start?" she asked.

"Today is good," he said. There was a crooked smile on his lips and a twinkle in his eyes.

"No, it's almost the end of the day. You won't get your days' worth. Why don't we officially start tomorrow?"

"Well, I'm already enjoying your company now, so I'd be the one taking advantage of you if we don't count today," he said.

"Take today as an activity between friends. It costs you nothing." It was the least that she could give him.

"So, can we spend dinner as friends as well?" he asked.

She felt the full blast of his charm, and a frisson of thrill went through her. In her panic, she nodded. Her throat was a little constricted for words.

Veren felt pleased with himself. He secured Anza's safety and gained her trust. Now, he found a way to get to know her and discover the best way to convince her to go back home to her parents.

He debated whether he should tell her father that he had

located Anza. But Manuu Soledad might preempt his plans and ruin his chance of fulfilling his mission in full. However, he would have to say something to Mr. Soledad later, or the man might just fly in and show up unannounced. He settled on sending him a text message to inform him that he was still looking for her. He got lucky when he chanced upon her so quickly—he would take advantage of that.

Edrigu Orzabal was a different matter. He didn't want to lie to his mentor. Edrigu knew he was flying to Basco. His mentor would assume that he was still looking for her today, and if he didn't call, Edrigu would assume there was nothing yet to report. Veren had a few hours before he needed to call him.

For now, he had to shower and change. He would meet Anza at six p.m., which gave him two hours to prepare for eventualities. While he had consumed enough human viscera to last him a week, it didn't hurt to cover all the bases. He must convince Anza before the week was out, because he would need to be back on the mainland to get his *sustenance*.

He sat down with his tablet to record the details of the day, his observations and what he learned about her so far. Anza was not what he expected. He assumed she would be bratty, and half-expected her to give up and go home before he could find her.

It was the foremost reason he was in a hurry to beat her to it. To find her was not enough of an accomplishment. He wanted to be instrumental to her decision to go home, so there would be no doubt he did his job to its fullest extent. He wanted to earn the resolution of the case, rather than get it resolved by default.

Based on what he saw from her yesterday, before he realised it was her, he thought she had grit and the fighting spirit to continue. This girl would not give up, and if he hadn't been lucky yesterday to have been in the right place at the right time, he probably would have run out of time looking for her.

Anza was still in a daze. She was breathless with the idea of having dinner with Veren. Her pulse hadn't slowed down even after she showered on autopilot. She wasn't even sure if she shampooed her hair. She relied on the texture of her tresses as she wriggled her fingers through, drying them upside down under the blast of the electric fan.

No boy, human or *Aswang*, had ever expressed this much interest in her before. And Veren was no longer a boy. She was unused to the attention shown to her by an attractive man, and it created this heady emotion.

Come to think of it, it's similar, although a little more intense than what I feel for Xandrei.

It was different because Veren was a stranger. He was just a decent guy who was sorry for her, and maybe she reminded him of his sister.

I don't even know if he has a sister.

With a sigh, she straightened up and flipped her hair back. The electric fan had dried it enough. The method gave her hair the body she wanted. She brushed it back into place, then secured the front pieces behind her head with a barrette. The baby hairs that grew around her face refused to be tamed without the aid of hairspray, so she gave up. This would have to do.

She couldn't behave around Veren like her giggly class-mates whenever they saw a boy. It would be humiliating. She would embarrass him and make their daily interactions awkward.

I must regard him as an older brother.

She would treat him like how she treated her cousin Xandrei, since there was nothing different in how Veren treated her from how her cousin did.

She spent the next couple of hours on an emotional seesaw between diverting herself from getting too excited about the dinner to imagining different scenarios, then chastising herself.

After a week, Veren could leave Basco, and she would have to focus on her goal to be independent. His friendship, the first-ever outside of her limited sphere, one formed naturally, was a good beginning to her new life. Hopefully, the memories that would come out of it would be worth remembering for the years to come.

She felt human already.

Veren was already waiting in the lobby when she arrived. It surprised her because she had left her room early. She was expecting to wait for him. He waved at her from the distance. A wide, delighted smile was on his face. He had changed into faded grey jeans and a dark blue T-shirt under a grey hoodie that was unzipped at the front. He looked carefree and young.

"Hungry?" he asked as she came closer.

She nodded in response. It was the best explanation for her being early. And it also explained why he was earlier than her. He must have been hungry, too.

He took her hand and pulled her with him. Like an older brother pulling his younger sister along. He walked her to a motorcycle parked at the side of the entrance and handed her a helmet.

She hesitated, unable to hide a slight alarm at the idea. A jolt of uncertainty struck her heart. She had never ridden a motorcycle before. It looked dangerous. She met Veren's gaze.

The helmet was still in his hand as he waited for her to accept it. His happy expression was both encouraging and challenging.

Take a chance, Anza. It's just a motorbike ride.

With a deep breath, she took the helmet and put it on under Veren's approving gaze. He fastened the strap under her chin. Her sense of bravery kicked up a notch, and the anticipation of the motorbike ride replaced some of her fears.

As she straddled the bike behind him, she didn't know where to attribute the added thrill that coursed through her, whether it was from the upcoming ride or the unfamiliar sensation of being pressed close to a male body—one that belonged to someone not related to her.

"Hold tight, Anza. And relax. Just lean on me. Don't worry, I'm an expert at motorbikes. I won't let you fall," Veren said over his shoulder.

He must have noticed my death grip around his middle.

"Ready?" he asked.

She nodded.

With a small jolt, they zoomed into the road towards the mystery destination of their dinner. She forgot to ask him where they were going.

Five minutes into the ride, she relaxed. Veren did not lie: he *was* an experienced rider. After the initial starting jolt, the drive smoothened into a fluid motion. The hum of the engine became noticeable to her, together with the feel of Veren's firm and warm back.

It was a brief ride, but with the newness of the experience, it felt drawn out yet fleeting. The surrounding sights went past in a blur of old houses, native vegetation, and people. Her focus was on the sensations rather than the view.

When they reached their destination, it came as a surprise.

She was expecting a simple neighbourhood eatery. Instead, the place looked like a must-go for tourists.

Perched atop a hill, the restaurant offered a stunning view of Vayang Rolling Hills. In the waning light, she could see the building was made of packed earth, bamboo, and wood. It had the thatched roof characteristic of the native Ivatan houses in the area. The flowering plants and green hedges that surrounded the restaurant compound gave it a homey yet magical quality.

The sea breeze that rolled from the ocean cooled the place. There was a small blackboard by the entrance that had the specials for the day: grilled flying fish served on Kabaya leaf, and coconut crabs cooked in coconut milk.

The wait staff ushered them to a table near the window. There were about eight tables in the restaurant, four already occupied. The air had a slight flavour of turmeric, coconut, banana leaves, and sea air.

"I don't know about you, but I find today's specials hard to resist. Do you like seafood?" Veren asked, his eyes gleaming.

"I love seafood. I've never had flying fish and coconut crab before," she said, unable to curb her own excitement.

"Okay, let's get those, and ... some Luñis," he said.

"What's a Luñis?" Everything on this island cuisine-wise was new to her, but that couldn't have put her off, as nothing could be stranger than what her *Aswang* family partook in regularly.

"It's an indigenous dish of preserved pork, usually served fried, crispy, and paired with turmeric rice," he replied.

"How do you know all this?" It amazed her that he knew so much about the island in such a short time.

"Internet searches. I do them before I visit any place," he said, a smug look on his face. "Did you not do the same before you came here?"

"No. My decision to come here was ... an impulse."

"Why? What brought you here? It seems such a long way away from where you were from—the south close to Batangas."

"I'll tell you tomorrow when I'm officially in your employ." She would avoid answering questions about her identity for as long as she could and evade it with every means she had.

He looked at her, eyes narrowed in speculation, then he shrugged his shoulders. "Fair enough."

He got back to perusing the menu. She did the same.

Veren was glad he had already chosen what he wanted to eat when he saw the blackboard earlier. He wasn't reading the menu—he was trying to sense Anza's mood. She came out relaxed, fresh-faced and every bit the sixteen year-old that she was. There was something about her that appealed to him—a mixture of vulnerability and fire. She made him want to tease her, challenge her to take chances, and keep her safe and take care of her in equal measure.

She was reluctant to get on the motorbike earlier. He expected her reaction. It was not the safest form of transportation for most people, and she was a sheltered young woman who was used to the chauffeured, four-wheel kind. He liked bikes but would have rented a car for her if there was one available. It was the spark of courage he saw in her earlier that made him goad her. He had a feeling she would accept his challenge.

And he was right.

He was glad to have chosen this restaurant. Anza did not expect it. He smiled to himself when he recalled her expression. She liked this place. He noticed that his efforts to develop her trust in him had kept her off-balanced and it was proving effective. She needed to reach the point where his words would have enough sway in her decisions. She needed to heed his advice to come home voluntarily.

"Are you ready to order?" he asked.

She said she was hungry earlier. She only had noodles for lunch, and because she was upset then, she might not have eaten well. As far as he knew, she only had a cup of coffee aside from that. She smiled and nodded at him, putting her menu down. He beckoned the server over and ordered both the coconut crab and the flying fish, plus an order of Luñis.

"What would you like to drink?" he asked.

She didn't respond. Instead, her eyes were full of speculation.

"Will you order a beer?" she asked.

"For you? No, you're too young." He wasn't about to corrupt her with bad habits.

"Not for me, for you," she said, her upper lip curled in mild annoyance.

That made him smile. That one action displayed sparks of her inner fire.

"Well, yeah, I am having a beer ..."

"I'd like to take a sip out of yours ... Just for the experience." Her tone was hopeful, like a little girl asking for ice cream, but the gleam of naughtiness in her eyes was adult.

"Ah, I guess that's okay. I'll give you a sip. But what would you like to drink?"

He felt pleased and somewhat guilty for enabling Anza, for allowing himself to be used to test her new independence, to sharpen her claws. On the plus side, this would deepen her trust in him.

"I will have Kalamansi juice," she said after perusing the drink menu.

The server came with their drinks five minutes later. She was looking expectantly at his beer, which arrived ice cold. Her glance flew to his face when he made no move to hand the bottle over. With a chuckle, he pushed it to her.

An excited giggle escaped her as she lifted the bottle to her lips too quickly. He didn't have time to warn her as she took a huge gulp and swallowed the icy liquid. She spluttered and snorted the beer out of her mouth and nose, her body wracked with coughs, her eyes watering.

He found it impossible not to laugh even as he patted her back gently and gave her his handkerchief. Anza glared at him through teary eyes. As her cough subsided, she took a sip of water from the glass he handed her. He held the bottom to control the amount that she could take. She didn't resist. That pleased him. Already, she trusted him more.

The server hovered with a rag to wipe the splatter of beer on the table, but he motioned him away. He wiped the table dry with the napkins himself. He didn't want Anza to be more embarrassed. Her cheeks were delightfully red as she looked across from him and saw the people on the next table watching her. The flush of colour spread to her face and neck.

"Are you alright?" he asked as she dabbed her cheeks and eyes with his handkerchief. Her coughing had stopped.

She nodded, looking mortified still. He grinned at her. He couldn't help it. She looked so adorable with her red-rimmed eyes, the flush of high colour on her face and neck, defiance in her jawline. She looked incandescent with life.

"What do you think of the beer?" He tried to keep his face straight.

"It was painful, especially up the nose." Her tone and expression went deadpan. Her lips quivered, and for a split second, he thought she would cry. His gaze flew to her eyes in alarm. Mirth sparkled in her eyes as she tried to stop herself. Their eyes met, and they both burst out laughing.

"You weren't supposed to snort the beer, Anza," he said after he calmed down, in a tone reminiscent of a professor.

"The beer had a mind of its own. I wanted it to go down my throat, but it travelled up instead," she said. The humour of the incident lingered in her gaze.

As he looked at her face, the inner fire he saw in her seemed to have set her alight from within. She glowed. At that moment, he had a glimpse of what she could look like when she had grown into her womanhood. And it kindled something in him that expanded in his chest.

He felt glad that he was here, with her, tonight.

Their server arrived with their food, breaking the electrified moment. The aroma of the grilled flying fish came with the fragrance of heated banana leaves and a hint of citrus. Their crabs looked deliciously rich, the orange shells bathed in coconut cream. The golden-brown pork dish looked crunchy and mouthwatering.

They tucked into their food in relative silence. Anza was hungry as he watched her eat with complete absorption and enjoyment. She savoured a new dish with singularity—she would put it in her mouth, close her eyes, inhale deep, then hum under her breath as if she was engaging all her senses in one go. Her eating habits entranced him.

She didn't just eat her food, she experienced it.

This revealed more than words ever could as to why she rebelled and ran away. Her thirst to experience life to the fullest was deep, and her family, without conscious thought, hindered it.

It amused him to see her suck the flesh out of the crab claws. Her delight in it was so contagious that he ended up copying her. It became a game of who slurped the loudest. This was the first time a meal transcended into an event. It etched itself into his memory.

The sparkle in her eyes told him all was right in her world at that moment. She was happy. It sent a glad note to his heart and with it a sliver of apprehension. She might get used to this human life and that would make it hard for him to convince her to come home to her parents, to their kind, their world, and its veiled existence.

With their bellies full of food and in their hearts, merriment, they capped the night with coffee and enjoyed it over at the lookout point. The rhythmic sound of the waves crashing on the shore, the slight chill in the air paired well with the hot coffee. The result was very calming.

"That was a wonderful dinner," Anza said, glancing up at him. "Thank you."

Her hair was down from its earlier ponytail. The elastic seemed unable to hold it in place. The wind whipped it about her face, making it a challenge for her to drink her coffee in peace. He couldn't resist lifting the strands off of her cheeks and mouth and tucking them behind her ears.

She handed her cup to him as she self-consciously gathered her hair back in a low ponytail. She tucked the shorter baby hairs that grew around her face behind her ears. In that instance, she looked like the sixteen year-old that she was, and he felt a twinge of regret. She was still a baby. And the object of his mission. It was unseemly for him to develop a crush on a high-school student.

This must be how a crush works—the object of your interest seems to blossom right before your eyes, making her more beautiful, more compelling every second.

"What was your favourite dish?" he asked, to keep his mind off its present preoccupation.

She paused, her head tilted, eyes narrowed. "Hmm ... I can't decide. I like them all."

"If you can order only one dish when we dine next time,

which among the three would you reorder?" He was unsure why he wanted to find out her answer to his question, but it felt essential.

"I think ... the crab," she replied with a smile.

He was reminded of their slurping game and smiled back. "Yes, me too. It's a pity that it's an endangered species and we can't eat them regularly." They had tried to reorder another, but the restaurant limited each table to one order.

"Yes, that's sad. But I heartily support that rule. It's for the good of the coconut crab population," she replied.

"Are you a rule-breaker or a law-abiding citizen?" He now faced her as he handed her coffee back.

That gave her pause, although her stance was still relaxed. She took a sip from her cup and sighed. The sound was like a breeze on a scorching afternoon.

"I've never broken a law. I've always abided by it ... but ..."

He waited for her to continue. She seemed unable to.

"But not today?" he suggested. He kept his expression non-judgmental. He wanted her to open up.

She looked thoughtfully at him, as if gauging if she could take the step of trusting him with her secrets.

"Exactly—not today," she said.

His heart jolted a beat faster. "So, will you tell me why you came to be here? Why you're so far away from home?" he asked, staring at her.

She tucked the strand of hair the breeze had freed from behind her ear before she replied. "I ran away from home and came here to learn ... independence."

"What made you run away?" He needed to understand what drove someone like her to leave a family who seemed to love her, to put herself at risk in an environment she was unfamiliar with.

"I can't tell you," she whispered.

She spoke as if her heart was tight. He knew she was hoping he would accept her response and leave it at that.

"Is it something that can't be resolved?"

"I don't know," she replied.

The sigh that preceded the words was heartfelt. He wanted to probe, but he couldn't press her. Not yet. Then a dreadful idea dawned on him. There might be another reason she left home; one they did not consider.

He frowned. "Anza, were you getting hurt? Are you in any danger?" He prayed it wasn't so.

She looked touched by his concern. And he was glad when she shook her head.

"No, Veren. I'm not in any danger. And I wasn't getting abused at home. I ... just can't live the same way. I'm different from them, and I have to face that fact. Eventually, I'll have to leave them anyway. I just want to have an early start and not get too dependent on their presence. It's better to do it now while I'm young and able," she said.

He knew it was the most she could tell him. It was very difficult not to reassure her that he understood what she was going through. Silence reigned between them as he digested what she revealed. Her cousin and her mother were right about her and what made her run away from home.

Anza looked up and was struck by the expression on Veren's face. It was like he just saw her for the first time. And yet the way he angled his head as he fixed her with a penetrating stare made her feel like a revelation to him.

"Do you not think your parents will be anxious about you?" Veren asked. His frown was etched with concern.

"I had planned to send word to them that I'm okay. Hopefully, it will suffice," she said.

"That wouldn't suffice. You're very young, and pardon me for saying so, but you don't strike me as someone who is used to this ... spartan kind of life," he said.

She couldn't contradict him. Mrs. Bassig made the same comment to her earlier, and it was her obvious naivete that convinced Mrs. Bassig to offer her a trainee position as front desk and guest relations officer for the next six months.

"Is it that obvious that I'm inexperienced?"

"Hell, yeah! You look like a child, a sheltered child," he said. His voice had increased in intensity. He sounded annoyed, almost angry.

"I'm not a child. I'm already sixteen. Most people call me a young woman!"

Veren sighed, reaching out to take her icy hands between his. He shook his head as if he regretted having raised his voice earlier.

"Anza, for most parents, sixteen is still a child. And you look younger than sixteen." His tone was gentler.

"Well, I can't help that I have baby face genes in me..." She felt like stomping her feet, but that would just prove his point. Instead, she pulled her hand from his and turned away.

There was silence from Veren. She waited for his comment, but there was none. And when she glanced back at him, his lips quivered from the effort not to grin.

"I suppose declaring that I'm an adult, then throwing a tantrum to prove it, is counterproductive," she said.

Veren grinned.

Her own smile broke through her lips and spread to her heart.

5 THE DEVELOPMENT

He had been staring at his phone for almost an hour now since he returned from walking Anza to her room. He had been trying to decide what to report to Edrigu. Why he put himself up to the goal of convincing Anza to go home was beyond him.

A call-in for his progress for the day was due, and he didn't want to lie. If he told Edrigu that he found Anza already, he might wonder why he had not told Anza's father about it. He could use Manuu Soledad's own desire to have Anza come home at her own choice as the reason, but Edrigu might point out that Manuu would want to do the convincing himself. All he had to do was let Manuu know Anza's location.

With Manuu, he could pretend that he misunderstood his instruction, but with Edrigu, there wouldn't be any ambiguity. If his mentor gave him an order, he could not go against it.

Unless ...

An idea came to him. He dialled Edrigu's number, pulse picking up. His mentor answered in two rings.

"Good evening, Veren. How are you coming along in Basco?" Edrigu's voice was clear despite the distance.

"I'm good, Sir. I just called in to report on my progress." He kept his tone controlled to tamp down his own uneasiness at the minor deceit he would play on his mentor.

"Okay. Do you have solid leads about Manuu's daughter's location?" Edrigu asked.

"Yes, Sir. I found her this afternoon," he replied.

"Wow! That was fast. Have you told Manuu? What is the arrangement? When are you due back here?" Edrigu's questions made his heart race.

"I have not told Mr. Soledad that I found her. Ms. Soledad still does not know I am an *Iztari*, and I'm afraid if she finds out, she will disappear again. Her father wants her to come home willingly and telling him might not achieve that—he might show up here and spook her away." He hoped his voice wouldn't give away his exaggeration of the facts. "And, if she disappears this time, we may not find her again."

Edrigu was silent on the other line. He had the impression that his mentor knew what he was doing. With luck, Edrigu would consider the logic in his explanation.

"So, you want to convince her yourself?" Edrigu asked. The tone of clarification made Veren's heart skip a beat. His mentor read his intention with ease.

"Yes, I was hoping to do that, Sir." He held his breath as he waited for Edrigu's response.

"Okay. So, what kind of help do you need from me?" Edrigu asked.

Veren felt his relief like a loosening of a tight band on his chest.

"Help me reassure Mr. Soledad that he need not worry about his daughter, that I can convince her to come home voluntarily," he said.

"How much time do you need to accomplish this?"

"A week, hopefully, since I would need to go to the mainland for *sustenance* by then," he replied.

"Okay. I'll take care of Manuu. In the meantime, I will give a heads-up to the *Sustenance Supply* in the mainland to prepare for your needs," Edrigu said. "Just in case."

"Thank you, Sir. I truly appreciate it." His chest loosened with relief.

"You're welcome," Edrigu said, then hung up.

He was sure, at that moment, that his mentor knew exactly what he was up to and was giving him the latitude to do so. He felt better and guiltier by the end of that conversation. He fell asleep justifying to himself that he just wanted to complete the mission in its entirety.

Anza had been running through the night's events again and again in her head. The exhilaration she experienced tonight was all new to her. The mental back and forth of being hopeful and cautious, in giving meaning to each word and action that was part of this experience, had kept her unbalanced.

This must be what having a crush is like—being in constant awareness of his presence, his words, and actions.

Veren was the first male human she had spent this much time with. Her father's rules had prevented her from forming friendships, even with her classmates, limiting her to brief conversations and tepid, trivial pleasantries. The warnings of potential separation pain when they *Transit* was never far from her mind.

She blamed her own inexperience for her susceptibility to Veren's attention. But her father did not raise an airhead, so it would be an insult to him if she allowed a crush to sway her within a few days of being independent. Veren may be human, but she was not about to exchange a dependency from one species to another.

Besides, depending on a man's affection as a source of joy would be counterproductive for her search for true happiness.

Tomorrow, I will look at all the actions and words of Veren to be nothing more than those from an older brother.

Or a good friend ...

No, an older brother ... Nothing could develop outside of a brother-sister relationship.

She walked into the lobby, expecting to see Veren, but he was nowhere. She was looking about for him when he came out of the gift shop at the corner. He was carrying a bottle of sunblock, which he handed to her.

"Are we going to the beach?" She looked at the bottle in her hand.

"We're going to a lighthouse. I don't know if the beach that comes with it is good for swimming, but I thought it best to be prepared," he said. "Do you want to get your swimsuit? Just in case it's possible to swim there?"

"I didn't bring one." There was a lake and a creek on their property, but like the previous trips, she was not expecting to swim, since her family always left her behind when they ventured into the woods.

Veren glanced at the gift shop, and she saw a rack of swimsuits inside. She stopped him before he turned back towards the shop.

"It's okay, I ... don't want to swim today. There will be other opportunities. We *are* on an island ..." She turned away and slid the sunblock in her backpack to avoid any more conversation about the topic.

Veren's eyes narrowed. He looked like he wanted to insist, but she stopped him with a question. "Shall we go?"

"We're leaving in a while. I'm still waiting for something," he said, a small smile on his face.

She nodded and sat down on the couch. She was a tad hungry but didn't think she would have enough time to order a sandwich. Veren might be on a schedule, and she didn't want to cause a delay.

A coffee shop worker came out with a small picnic basket just as she was thinking to buy a bottle of water to tide her over. She handed the basket to Veren, who thanked her with a smile. The girl blushed and tittered.

"Shall we?" Veren inclined his head to her, and she followed him out to where he had parked his motorbike. He secured the basket at the back of the bike while she picked up the helmet she used the day before and put it on.

"Do you have a jacket?" Veren looked at her flimsy T-shirt.

She shook her head. Veren took off his own backpack and fished out a long-sleeved shirt.

"Put this on—the ride is long. You'll get cold," he said.

He helped her slide her backpack off, holding the cotton shirt as she pushed her arm through the sleeves. It was soft and well-worn. It carried his natural fragrance and something citrusy. The man smelled good ... and familiar. Yet, she couldn't identify it.

She was picking through the catalogue of scents in her memory when Veren grasped the front of the shirt and buttoned her up into it like a child. His action startled her into stillness, allowing him to do the task quickly.

The sleeves seemed a foot longer than her arms when she

held it up. Veren grinned and folded it back to allow her fingers to show.

"Shall we?" He nudged her chin with a knuckle. She nodded and followed, straddling the bike behind him.

I'm a little sister to him.

He's like the big brother I never had.

She repeated the words to herself as they zoomed along the country road, her arms wrapped around his waist, her thumbs hooked on his belt loops.

They drove through cliff-side roads that offered stunning views of the sea, and interior rural streets that oozed with quaintness. They zipped past towns humming with country life: women sweeping front lawns and hanging laundry; kids playing with sticks and well-used traditional toys; men walking with a purpose towards somewhere, and domestic animals and livestock meandering about.

It was such a simple, very human existence. She was both sad and glad to be in the middle of it. Life on this island contrasted sharply with her previous one. It was almost poetic that she had ended up here to start her new life as a human. It was a perfect representation of back to basic and starting from the bottom.

But if she was to start her life with this new beginning, she could not have chosen a more appropriate location. She was far safer here than if she had chosen the big city. A simpler life was easier to achieve among simple people and surroundings.

The ride took three hours. Her butt went numb, her throat dry, her stomach protested in hunger, yet she didn't ask for a break. She didn't want to inconvenience Veren. Her job was to be his companion, not a dependent. She was wondering how much longer the trip was going to take when they turned right into one of the country roads, and there it was: the Basco Lighthouse.

It gleamed white from the distance, standing solitary and imposing at the edge of a hill. It reminded her of the immobile Beefeater that guarded the Tower of London. Maybe because it appeared as dependable? This concrete guard looked like it watched and waited for passing ships in perfect patience for decades.

Their bike purred to a halt by the parking area in front of a building with a blue roof. It was a closed café. She hopped off to allow Veren to kick open the bike stand and secure it in place, then she removed her helmet to better view her surroundings. The sea, a deep aquamarine that blended into the intense blue of the sky. The hills were lush and emerald, like undulating pillows of vegetation.

And the air tasted of sea salt and adventure.

On impulse, she ran closer to the safety railing that protected the visitors from falling off the cliff. A wooden stairway with thick ropes for support snaked across the face of the hillside down to the beach.

The exceptional beauty and serenity of the scene drew her eyes in. The sound of the waves in a perpetual race to the shore, the bright blue sky that forced her to squint, and the light breeze that swept in from the sea soothed her ragged spirit. It seemed like the world had given her permission to dare. To live.

She looked back to check where Veren was. He had untied the basket from behind the bike and carried it with him as he approached her. He led her towards the lighthouse. They stopped by the grassy area in front of the circular tower. Veren unfolded a fabric she recognised to be a tablecloth from the coffee shop at their lobby. He knelt and unloaded the contents of the basket: bottled water, sandwiches, and packed garden salad.

"Let's eat first." He tugged at her hand to make her sit down. She slumped beside him, almost landing on his lap.

Veren chuckled and gave her a bottle of water, cap loosened. She drank it down to half and sighed in relief as the cool liquid soaked the parched tissues of her throat.

"I figured you were dehydrated," he said. Amusement glittered in his eyes.

"How could you tell?" She picked up a sandwich.

"Your lips were dry." He tapped the bow of her lips with a gentle finger.

Her gaze flew to his as her fingers covered her lips in defence. "It was a long ... and windy ride," she mumbled, focusing her gaze on the sandwich in her hands to will away the heat that bloomed on her cheeks.

It was a long roll that looked like a hotdog bun. She opened it to examine the filling. The scent of lemon and dill wafted from it. By the look of it, this was a lobster roll sandwich, the specialty of the coffee shop, but one she had yet to try.

"Eat. That looks delicious," Veren said. He was holding a big cheeseburger.

She took a bite and almost moaned—the chilled lobster meat was fresh and sweet, with a hint of mayonnaise, celery, lemon juice, and dill. The bread was soft and the combination of flavours sublime.

Veren shook his head at her, his expression a mixture of regret and amusement as he took a bite of his burger. She realised Veren might have ordered the lobster roll for himself, and she took what she wanted without care, without asking him.

"Oh, did you want this?" She felt guilty that she hadn't even asked Veren before she took the lobster roll.

He laughed. "It doesn't matter. It's just ... your appetite is contagious."

"No, truly, we can share. I *cannot* finish this." She set down the bun to search for a knife to cut the roll in half. Veren stayed her movement, his cool hand on hers.

"No need to slice it. Eat and enjoy it. I'll finish the leftovers if there are any," he said.

"Won't that be off-putting ... to eat my leftovers?" she asked.

"You don't have rabies, so I'm not worried," he said. He stopped her protest by lifting her chin to close her mouth. "Stop arguing, little one. Just eat. I know you didn't have breakfast this morning."

Little one?

"How did you know?" She hoped she didn't look starved.

"I asked. They said you hadn't come down to breakfast."

"Oh ..."

She didn't know what to think about that. Veren had a mischievous twinkle in his eyes as he continued to eat. She followed his lead and finished her lobster roll.

Little one, really?

Like a puppy?

Veren watched Anza surreptitiously. She ate like a child, with full enjoyment. She was prim and proper when she was conscious of what she was doing, as if she had to stop herself from being too enthusiastic, from immersing herself in the moment. Yet, when she forgot herself, when the experience overcame her reserve, she soaked it all in, full senses deep.

It was stirring to behold.

Is this how she lived her life? Like a flame trapped in a glass jar, slowly suffocating at the lack of oxygen?

Anza reminded him of the young elephant he saw in Thailand a few years ago. It grew up tied to a metal pole, so it got accustomed to the limited movement of the length its leash allowed. The animal was so used to being bound that it stayed within that range even though it had doubled in size and could uproot the pole if it so desired.

Anza was the elephant who walked beyond the range and uprooted the pole. However, the experience was so new to her that it scared her. She could still feel the imaginary leash of the *Vis* world and its restrictive power. She would never be free until the muscle memory of being reined in faded and left her completely. That would require exposure to the other side of her world, beyond her comfort zone and into unknown dangers.

In that moment, Veren could empathise with Manuu Soledad.

Anza roused something soft and intense in him, a sense of protectiveness that he had never felt for anyone before. She was like a kitten, all fluffy fur and claws; like a filly, ready to bolt anytime she got spooked. And Anza was a hair's breadth away from bolting deeper into a surrounding she was unfamiliar with.

Anza reclined on the picnic cloth, stretched her arms over-head, and arched her back. Her actions were almost feline. He realised she must have been sore from the ride. She was rigid that whole time, despite the relaxed hold she had around his waist. It disappointed him that she wasn't comfortable enough to lean on him. But then, they had only known each other for less than twenty-four hours. It would be odd if she lacked caution.

With her eyes closed, he could observe her face. She looked very young, a bud still far from full bloom. Her youthful features, her size, her physique, her vulnerability called to his masculine protective instinct. He understood why her father sheltered her the way he did.

Anza stirred as he was putting away the remnants of their lunch. She got up and collected the cloth, folded and placed it into the basket. She was going to take it to the bike, but he took her by the hand and towed her toward the lighthouse. He placed the basket on a wooden bench by the circular stairs.

"Ready?" He smiled at her and pointed to the top of the tower.

"We can go up?" Her eyes rounded with undisguised excitement.

"Yes, we can. The view is best on the top."

She hesitated for a moment, gazing up. Her expression was a mixture of apprehension and thrill.

"Let's go." He tugged more firmly at her hand and made her choice easier.

With a giggle, she followed him up the narrow, winding stairs to the top. Their ascent was rushed. Halfway through, Anza stopped and gripped her sides, bent at the waist.

"Hang on," she gasped. Her face was flushed and glistening.

He gave her a couple of minutes' rest. Then, he pulled at her hand and said, "Hurry, while we have the lighthouse to ourselves. You can take pictures to your heart's content."

"How do you know I enjoy taking pictures," she asked, curious but without even not a tinge of suspicion.

Oops!

"Don't all teenagers?" He kept his tone neutral. Anza trusted him, and he needed to keep that trust. "Don't you have any social media?"

"Sure, I do, but it's private. Only for my consumption," she replied.

The familiar sadness flashed in her eyes.

"Don't you have followers?" he asked. He wanted to keep her talking. They were in the last five steps to the top.

She shook her head.

"Will you allow me to follow you online?" He made room

for her to step onto the platform, to the view. It unfolded before her, leaving her mouth agape, eyes wide.

"Wow!" she breathed out.

That drew a wide smile from Veren. Her delight gave him pleasure.

"Wow, indeed!" he said, following her gaze towards the horizon.

The sun was no longer overhead. The sky, where gaps between patches of thick clouds showed, was a clear blue, but he could sense an oncoming rain. He felt the change of pressure in the atmosphere and smelled it in the air. Anza had better take her photos soon.

A quiet sigh escaped Anza's lips, and regret flashed in her eyes. He realised that, since he met her, he had never seen her use her cell phone.

"Don't you want to take pictures?"

"No." She shook her head. There was a slight downturn at the corner of her lips. "It's all right. My social media isn't that important right now."

"You don't have to post it until you're ready." He wanted to capture this moment for her. "It may be a long time before we return here, so take the pictures now."

She looked even more crestfallen. "I don't want to turn my phone on," she said.

"Why?" He frowned.

"My father could be tracking my phone ..."

It surprised him that she knew about how cell phones worked. He didn't expect it. Also, she was right. The *Iztari* office was tracking the transmission from her phone. Once again, he felt chagrined at his quick misjudgment of her capabilities.

He took out his own phone and handed it to her.

"What's this for?" Her eyebrows quirked.

"Use mine. And click away," he said. "I'll transfer the photos to your phone later."

"Oh, thank you!" On impulse, she bounced on her feet and launched herself into his arms.

"You're welcome." He hugged her back. The jolt in his heart made him uncomfortable. "Now go, while the light is good. The clouds are rolling in ..." He pointed at the sky.

"Yes, boss!" She gave him a gleeful salute and a wide smile. Her face beamed with pure joy.

Anza spent the next fifteen minutes taking shot after shot. She deleted those that didn't meet her standards and showed him the images she liked. Her innate talent for photography was on full display.

"Are we going somewhere else after here?" she asked as she handed him his phone.

"No," he said, sliding the phone in his pocket. "Sunset is beautiful here. The locals highly recommend it."

"That would be awesome," she said, eyes lit up once again.

"Let's hope the rain doesn't come before that."

Luck was with them. The rain came as the sun sank across the horizon. Anza had just finished taking photos.

It started as a drizzle, then turned into a sudden downpour. The wind drove the rain towards them and forced them inside the lighthouse for shelter. They sat together on the floor by the glass window, as the dark columns of rain undulated with the wind and lashed against the transparent barrier.

Rainwater had soaked Anza's jeans, and the hem of the shirt he loaned her. Within minutes, she was shivering. The tremors that ran down her slim body travelled from her shoulders to his, where they touched.

"You're cold," he said, and pulled her closer to keep her warm. His arm curved around her.

Her discomfort was significant enough that she didn't resist. In fact, she gladly leaned into him, sighing as she did. He anchored her better, her head cradled in the crook of his arm and shoulder, her cheek pressed against his chest.

The hum of the wind and the hiss of the downpour was hypnotic. Mother nature expressed its raw power in the churning waters of the sea, by the vertical drive of the wind, and the darkening of the sky. Veren knew Anza had dozed off. Her weight had settled on him. He centred her body and head on his chest, to make her more comfortable.

The rain droned on for hours. With her limp, warm body nestled against his, both of his arms around her, a cocoon of contentment enveloped him. He was at peace. He held her to him, this delicate creature with the tensile strength of titanium now temporarily in his keeping.

Gladness seeped into his soul and lulled him to sleep.

Anza surfaced from her nap in slow degrees. Her awareness first centred on a familiar scent, then the warm, hard flesh under her cheek, and a steady beating of a heart. It took her a moment to realise she was half reclined on Veren, his arm curved around her.

He was still asleep. She was reluctant to leave the comfort of his arms, but she eased herself out, trying not to wake him. She sat up and looked around—they were on the floor, leaned against the concrete wall of the lighthouse.

The slow flash of the light overhead reminded her of the cameras of old. The glass window mirrored her image back at her in intermittent flashes. It showed her hair in disarray. She pulled the hair tie off, then combed her fingers through her tresses, massaging her scalp.

The rain had stopped. The air smelled salty from the sea and tasted sweet from the wet grass. They should probably be heading home now. It was already dark, their ride was long, and she was hungry. Maybe she could ask Veren to stop by a convenience store for something to eat and drink. She gave Veren a gentle prod to rouse him.

"Hmm?" He blinked awake, looking up at her. He seemed disoriented and stared at her for a while.

"Shouldn't we go now? We have a long way to go," she whispered.

"Don't you want to wait for dawn? You can take photos of the sunrise to match your sunset shots," he murmured. Then he sat up and stretched his long limbs, a slight wince on his face.

"I would if I wasn't so hungry," she replied, and got up. Blood rushed to the numb places in her limbs, making her groan. "Pins and needles ..."

That made Veren smile.

"Do you think we can stop by somewhere for food?" She asked this to distract him from her embarrassment.

Veren's smile turned indulgent. He glanced at his watch. "I can do better. There's a cafe nearby." He jumped up and helped steady her on her feet.

"The blue and white building?" She gathered her hair back to tie it in a ponytail. "Isn't that closed?"

"It opens at 6 p.m.," he said, then stayed her hand. "Leave your hair down—it will help keep you warm." With a light touch, he smoothed the strands away from her face.

She found the affectionate gesture sweet.

Hand in hand, they walked down the circular stairs. They were the only two souls in the lighthouse. The weather discouraged tourists. The picnic basket was where they had left it, the motorbike still at the front of the cafe that was now open. A white car was parked nearby. After securing their basket on the bike, they proceeded inside.

There were three people in the cafe, two boys and a girl. They all swivelled and gaped at Veren and her as they walked in. She felt self-conscious, as the two boys' interest was fixed at her. She glanced up at Veren. His face was impassive, but he was looking at the boys as well. A slight tension emanated from him. Veren seemed wary and on guard.

The server greeted and ushered them to a table at the other end of the room. Veren pulled the chair where she could see the three in her peripheral vision. The guys were still looking at her. Veren sat beside her with a direct vantage point to the other table. His relaxed pose was misleading.

She wanted to look at the other table, to see what had caused his stress, but she didn't want to be obvious about it. The menu proved to be a useful shield, as she peered at them from behind it. The boys were still throwing glances her way.

She then noticed the girl with them had her eyes on Veren. She was older than her, with waist-length, shiny, straight hair and a self-confidence that made her feel uneasy. Her interest in Veren was as obvious as the interest her companions directed at her.

A stirring of animosity against the woman rose in her. She glanced at Veren. He was busy reading the menu, uninterested in the woman's gaze from across the room.

"What would you like to have, little one?" Veren asked, his eyes still on the menu. "How starved are you?"

She was, earlier. At the moment, her annoyance had lessened her appetite. But she wouldn't let the other woman ruin her dinner.

"Very," she said, "I would like this one," She pointed to the chicken dish on her menu.

He lowered his menu and looked at what she pointed at. "Okay. Is that enough?" he asked. His gaze went back to his menu after a cursory glance at hers. "No soup or salad?"

"No. The chicken is enough." The bite of satisfaction lessened her growing irritation. Veren didn't even glance in the woman's direction.

Veren signalled the server over and placed their order. She kept her eyes on him as she thought of ways to keep Veren from exchanging looks with the woman ogling him. The odious girl was now waiting for a chance to catch his eye, a small, ready smile on her face.

"You look irate, little one," Veren said. He reached over and picked up a lock of her hair and tickled the side of her nose with it. "Is that hang-ger?" His tone was teasing.

"Hang-ger?" She frowned in confusion. "You mean hunger?"

"No. Hang-ger. Hunger-induced rage." His eyes twinkled in mischief.

"Oh ... No, I'm not ..." Anza began, her temper heated. She realised it was a better explanation for her attitude, "I guess I am." She smiled at him apologetically.

"A bit of patience, little one," Veren chuckled.

He reached out and playfully pinched her cheek. Pleased with their exchange, her brain scrambled for ways to keep him engaged. None of her previous experiences with her father or cousin Xandrei seemed applicable. She had never had to manipulate her father or cousin to keep their attention on her. Then she remembered their deal.

"Don't I owe you stories for the meals?" she asked.

"Oh, yeah." Veren's smile widened. He looked pleased to be reminded of it.

"So, what would you like to know?" She was thrilled her ploy worked.

"Tell me about your childhood." Veren scooted his chair closer, an encouraging smile on his face.

She hesitated for a bit as she thought how much she could divulge without giving too much, without revealing her true identity.

"I'm an only child. My mother died of birth complications. My dad raised me alone for the first three years of my life, and then he married my stepmom. I call her *Momstie*," she began. She paused as the server arrived with their drinks. She wanted no one else to hear of her life story.

"Momstie?" Veren asked as he unwrapped the straw and pushed it into his drink.

"Ah ... Momstie, short for stepmom ..."

Veren nodded. He seemed impressed with the nickname.

"How was your relationship with your parents? Your dad, in particular." He blew on his coffee.

"It's a great relationship. My dad doted on me, but he was ... overprotective." She stirred the straw in her iced tea.

"How so?"

She felt a twinge of guilt at the thought of talking about her father to a stranger. She sighed, "I'm not allowed to make friends, not even with my classmates."

"You have no friends of your own age?" Veren's focus was solely on her now.

"None ... Just my cousin, rather, my step-cousin Xandrei. He's eighteen. He's the only one I'm ... close to," she said.

"Did your cousin know?" he asked, his expression appraising. "Your plan to run away, I mean."

She shook her head. "No, he's overprotective as well. He would have told Momstie." She took a sip of the iced tea to loosen the knot in her chest, buying time should he ask for more details. As a compulsion, she reached out for the paper straw covering; the flame of the lit candle on their table beckoned.

"Okay." Veren seemed to understand. He reached out and covered her fidgeting fingers with his. "How about your step-mom? Do you get along with her?"

She nodded. "Yes—she treats me like her real daughter. Momstie is cool. Nothing bothers her. In short, we're very different."

Veren said nothing. He just continued to look at her and seemed to wait for her next words.

The arrival of their food interrupted their conversation. Veren's eyebrows knitted in a quick reaction, but his face became a pleasant mask when he turned to the server.

The tone of their dinner changed. Their interaction had always been lighthearted, but now there was a depth, an added layer to their relationship. It was almost tangible, the finest of threads, yet strong. She waited for him to ask questions, to cue her to return to their previous topic, but he kept their conversation friendly and casual.

Veren ordered grilled lobster for himself. It reminded her that she stole his lobster roll sandwich earlier.

"I'm sorry ..." She felt driven to apologise again.

Veren looked up in surprise. "For what?"

"I took your lobster roll this morning." She pointed to his dish.

He shrugged. "It's no big deal. Actually, after seeing you eat the roll, it made me crave lobster." He scooped a chunk from the shell, dipped it in the lemon butter sauce, and popped it into his mouth. "Oh ... that is good ..." His voice deepened in appreciation.

"So, you really bought the roll for me, and the burger for yourself?" she persisted, wanting reassurance.

Veren chewed and swallowed before he replied with, "I bought both for either of us. If you had chosen the burger, I would have happily eaten the lobster. It was a simple matter of getting something I thought we would both like."

"Really? Are you—"

He cut her off. "Anza, eat your food. It's getting cold."

She smiled at him. In return, he gave the lock of her hair a slight tug and continued with his meal. There was a noticeable increase in the camaraderie between them during the rest of the dinner. They shared each other's food. She cut him a portion of her chicken and placed it on his plate. He reciprocated with his lobster but insisted she take a bite from his fork.

In her head, that last act could be sexy and romantic, just like in the movies.

Or platonic, like a big brother feeding his kid sister.

With her luck, it was probably the latter.

With two steaming cups of takeaway coffee, Veren drew Anza to her feet. The coffee shop would close soon. They would drink their coffee outside where they had lunch earlier. As Veren opened the door, a blast of frigid night air hit him. Behind him, Anza shivered.

He gave Anza the coffee cups to hold and pulled her into his jacket. Anza sighed, and it made him smile. They made their way back to the patch of grass in front of the lighthouse with a brief stop by their bike. He took the tablecloth from the picnic basket and tucked it under his jacket.

The downpour left the grounds wet. The tablecloth would not have offered protection. They ended up huddled on a dry patch atop a low boulder, their backs against the stone walls of the caretaker's house. The structure shielded them from the icy wind that swept inland from the sea.

"What brought you here in Batanes?" Anza asked as she blew on her hot coffee.

He took a sip before he answered. "Nothing in particular. Part of a bucket list ..." He wanted to avoid this topic. He didn't want to lie to her. It was a good thing she was too inexperienced to know how to probe for information.

Anza looked up from her cup and stared at him. "Will you tell me about your childhood?" she asked.

Fuck!

His heart leaped at the question. No one had asked him that question for years.

"Not much to tell. I was an orphan," he said. "My mentor took me under his wing when I was five, sent me to school, then gave me a job. He gave me everything a young person with no parents needs to survive and thrive." He adopted a relaxed posture to hide the fact that discussing his past was not a pleasant subject for him.

She didn't seem convinced by his facade. There was a frown on her face, but her eyes were devoid of her usual emotions. He couldn't tell what she was thinking. His little one had learned to mask her feelings.

Not good.

"It must have been hard," she said, her eyes never leaving him.

Darn!

He took a deep breath before responding. "Yes, I guess it was." Giving brief replies might discourage her from asking for more.

"So, what do you do now?" she asked, her head inclined to the side.

Holy Aquila! She's persistent.

He took a big gulp of his lukewarm coffee to buy time to plan his response.

"I'm in between jobs," he said. That was technically true. "I return to my new one in a month," he added.

"A month? Are you staying here for that long?" Anza was looking at her own cooling cup, her voice stilted.

"Maybe ... although it depends," he replied to the top of her head. He wished he could see her expression.

"On what? I thought this trip was part of your bucket list."

Wish granted—she was looking at him again.

"Well, the items in my bucket list are not simple, one-layered things to be ticked off," he replied.

Anza's nod was slow, but whether she accepted and understood what he said was unclear. It seemed to be an automatic action she did when she was trying to make sense of the information she received.

They both turned towards some voices that were coming closer to them. The group of humans at the coffee shop were now going their way. Anza glanced at Veren with a frown. She couldn't make out what they were saying. Thanks to his superior hearing, the conversation of the incoming party was clear. The three were looking for them. The boys were keen on meeting Anza, and the girl was interested in him.

He sighed. They would have to deal with these juveniles unless they left the lighthouse. But he promised Anza the sunrise ...

"Oh ... do you think they're coming this way?" Anza asked, her nose wrinkled in disapproval.

"I'm afraid so, little one. You'll have to put effort into being sociable," he said.

She shook her head. He pulled her closer in a mock headlock.

"I don't know how to be sociable," she replied from beneath his arm, then untangled herself from his hold. He could almost imagine her pouting, except she wasn't the pouting kind.

"Then this is a good time to learn," he said, and released her.

Anza combed her hair back and twisted to face him. There was a worried crease on her brow and fear in her eyes.

"You did well with me. You weren't shy," he reminded her.

Her frown deepened. "You're different. You didn't give me time to think, and I forgot I didn't know how to be sociable," she said.

"Well, do what you did with me. Just answer their questions ... and don't frown." He touched her forehead to ease the creases. "And I'm here. I'll help you."

Three minutes later, the group caught up to them.

"Hi, guys! Are you waiting for the sunrise, too?" The only girl in the group was leading the pack. She wore a wide, friendly smile.

"Yes," he answered casually.

He surveyed the group standing ten feet away. She was carrying two bottled waters, one in each hand. The guy behind her was carrying an extra bottle. A quick look at the bottle caps told him that both were unopened.

"Can we join you?" she asked, then paused right in front of him. Her question was just for him, despite the word 'we'. She stood with a stance seemingly meant to emphasise her curvaceous hips. The girl apparently knew she possessed a splendid figure and was using it to her advantage.

Veren glanced at Anza to make sure she was okay. Her face showed no emotion, but he could feel the slight tension emanating from her. He almost said no.

"Sure, join us." He gestured toward the space in front of them. The soldier in him wanted them where he could see them.

"I'm Charisse," the girl said, waving with the bottle in her hand.

"I'm Veren."

"Hi—I'm Anza," Anza said. The tension in her shoulders increased, but her voice was calm.

"I'm Diego," the taller of the two boys said. He had short shorn hair at the back and the sides, but the front was longer and styled up. His smile revealed a pair of dimples and nice teeth.

"Hey—I'm Charlie," the other boy said. This one had longer, slicked-back hair. "Would you like some water?" Charlie asked, offering the bottle in his hand to Anza.

Veren intercepted it. He wanted to make sure it was safe. The bottle was chilled. He unscrewed the cap and handed it to Anza.

The boy's expression was telling. Charlie was unsure of how to react to Veren's protective gesture. Veren didn't care—he wanted this boy pre-warned that he was here to protect Anza.

"Thank you," Anza said, directing her remark to Charlie.

"Can we sit with you?" Charisse asked. She eyed the space in between Anza and him. She seemed to want him to scoot a little, to make room for her.

He nodded, but before Charisse could act on it, Anza moved nearer and covered that coveted gap. She took the option away and made her opinion about the situation clear.

Charisse, to her credit, was unfazed. She sat in front of him, cross-legged, her back to the view. The two boys copied her. The rock could only accommodate two-and-a-half people. Both Diego and Charlie positioned themselves right in front of Anza.

Time to do due diligence on the three. "So, where are you guys from?"

"We're from Baguio," Charisse replied with a disarming

full smile. "Diego and I are cousins. Charlie here is Diego's friend, frat brother, and my classmate."

"What brought you here?" Veren asked.

"We're on holiday," Charisse replied. Her free hand now played with her own hair, twirling it like most young women do when trying to be overtly feminine.

"Which school do you go to?" Anza's question sounded relaxed.

He glanced at her and noticed that her posture was rigid and almost defensive. Anza was asserting herself. His little one was flexing her confidence muscle.

"Oh, U.P. Baguio," Charisse said. She looked at Anza for the first time, her smile tight at the corners. The girl clearly saw Anza as competition.

"How about you, Anza? Which school do you go to?" Diego asked, his tone open and friendly.

"I don't know yet. I haven't decided where to go," Anza replied.

His little one was cool under pressure. When it came to hiding her background, Anza's years of practice as an *Erdia* showed.

"So, are you from here, or are you visiting like we are?" Charlie asked, glancing at Diego, a challenge in his gaze.

Veren could read the competition between the two boys. And he didn't like it. Their antics to win her regard might prove enough of an inducement for a young girl like Anza to want to stay with the humans longer.

"We're visiting." Anza's curt reply was guarded, not encouraging.

Veren inwardly smiled. So far, the boys hadn't enticed her. She was too inexperienced to use their attraction to her to her full advantage.

"How long are you here for?" Charisse asked. Her gentle touch on his knee ensured that he would look at her.

He turned to Charisse, who was smiling at him as she waited for his reply. Anza's interest in his reply to Charisse's question gleamed in her gaze, which had turned on him.

"For however long it takes to accomplish what we want to do here," he replied, answering for them both.

"Are you ... together?" Charisse's asked, her tone tentative, one eyebrow arched.

It was clear to him that she wanted to know her chances. The two boys were also keen to find out if Anza was available. He chose to misunderstand the question. He wasn't about to divulge the nature of their relationship.

"Yes. We came here together," he replied, and glanced at Anza.

Anza gave him a slow blink of annoyance. A quiet huff followed as she turned to Diego. He was unsure what caused her ire—he thought that she wouldn't want her circumstance known to strangers.

"So, Anza, are you going to University this coming school year?" Diego asked, outwardly glad to have her looking at him.

She shook her head. "11th grade."

"Oh, you're about ... 17?" Diego asked. "I'm 18, turning 19."

"I'm sixteen." Anza's admission came out reluctantly.

"Wow, you must have started school early," Charlie interjected, unwilling to stay in the background.

"No, I skipped first grade." Anza's response was automatic. That was news to Veren. Her records didn't mention it.

"You must be smart, then." Charlie's comment had a hint of condescension.

Veren felt Anza's defensive barriers rise, annoyance in her eyes. His little one had claws and was preparing to use them. Charlie was still smiling at her, unaware of the effects of his words. *This would be interesting to watch.*

"There are worse things than being smart," Anza said, her tone clipped.

Charlie's face fell as he realised his mistake.

"I agree with Anza. Being a basketball jock, for one." Diego wisely picked up the opening that Charlie's gaffe created, and gave Anza a conspiratorial smile.

Anza smiled back at him. Diego scored a point there. Veren felt a kick of irritation and a stirring of dislike towards Diego.

A cool breeze swept over them, making Anza shiver. She was the only one among them unprepared for the cold temperature. The thin shirt he loaned her was not enough to keep the chill away.

"Do you want my jacket, Anza?" Charlie offered, poised to remove his windbreaker, and redeem himself from the earlier mistake.

"There's no need," Veren said, stopping Charlie. He took the picnic cloth tucked inside his jacket, shook it out, and draped it over Anza's shoulder. The cloth retained the heat from his body. He took advantage of the opportunity and placed his arm around her, pulling her closer to him.

He could better protect her like this.

6 IN KEEPERSHIP

I f I was a full Vis, a true Aswang with shape-shifting skills, my animal form would be a cat. No doubt about it.

The cosiness of being cradled by Veren was purr-inducing, and she would have purred if she had been capable of it. His left arm was draped behind her, cushioning her back against the stone wall. She had laid her head on his chest. He smelled of that unidentified yet familiar scent of himself and night air. She closed her eyes to savour and drown her senses with the sensation of being close to him. It was also useful to pretend to doze off to avoid engaging with the three people who invaded their private moment.

She was comfortable, both inside and out. She could stay like this until morning. No conversations, just being together. The sound of the waves, the cool breeze that wafted from the sea, and the comfortable semi-darkness had a mellowing effect on her. Nothing Charisse or Charlie could say or do tonight could rouse her temper.

"Aww ... she's so sweet. The poor kid fell asleep," cooed Charisse.

Except that.

"Has she?" Veren asked with laughter in his voice.

She knew Veren was aware that she wasn't sleeping, that she just didn't want to socialise and this was her means of escape. The tension in her body would have been impossible for him to ignore.

A lull in the conversation followed. Her hair tingled at the sensation of eyes resting on her. Perhaps they were making sure she was indeed asleep.

"What do you do, bro?" Diego asked, breaking the silence.

Anza thought, *That's a good question.* She also wanted to know Veren's answer.

"I'm into asset recovery," Veren replied, a hint of mirth in his tone.

Asset recovery? That made her peek under her lashes.

"Cool ..." Diego clearly didn't know what Veren meant.

"You're in finance, then?" Charlie piped in.

"Not quite."

Veren's reply made her want to press him for more explanation herself, but she couldn't because she was pretending to be asleep.

"What type of assets do you recover? Properties? Vehicles?" Charlie persisted.

"Only those of extreme value," Veren replied. He rearranged the cloth that had slid down her back.

She wondered what valuables he was referring to. His response to the question didn't make his position clear.

"How long have you three been friends?" Veren asked, effectively ending that topic.

She could almost see his raised eyebrow, a habit of his when asking questions.

"Years," Charisse replied. "Diego and I have hung out together since grade school. Charlie and I met two years ago through Diego." Charisse sounded glad to be directly conversing with Veren.

She heard Charisse shift in her position, maybe to find a more comfortable one, or to move closer to Veren.

"Are you and Anza related by blood?" Charisse's question was bold and direct.

Veren stiffened. Either it surprised him, or he didn't like the question.

"We're not." Veren's response was curt. It discouraged further probing.

She wondered if Veren's clipped response told Charisse he wasn't about to divulge any information about them. Hopefully, the woman was smart enough to pick up on the nuance.

"What *is* your relationship with her?" Charisse asked.

Apparently not.

"At the moment, I'm her keeper," Veren said. The muscle in his arm flexed. It felt like it tightened around her.

"Keeper? What is that? Like a babysitter?" There was a slight smirk in her tone.

"Or a bodyguard?" Diego asked.

"Anza doesn't need a sitter, and she can take care of herself," Veren said.

There was a tinge of pride in his voice, and a touch of disbelief, like it was a revelation to himself. It warmed her insides.

"So, what does it mean to be her keeper?" Charisse persisted.

"I'll let Anza answer that," Veren replied, evading the question.

"But she's asleep ... Can you just tell us?" Charisse cajoled.

Under her lashes, she saw Charisse reach out to touch Veren's knee. She wanted to slap it away, and didn't realise her hand, sandwiched between them, was clenched until Veren chuckled and squeezed her shoulder.

Veren shook his head. "No, that would betray our keeper-ship," he replied, chuckling.

Charisse released a slow breath of frustration. "How old are you, Veren?" she asked.

"I'm ... 23," he replied, surprised at the turn of Charisse's question.

"I'm turning 20," Charisse said, with a note of glee. "We only have three years' age difference between us," she continued. "My cousin and Charlie are closer to Anza's age," she added when Veren didn't respond.

Anza sensed Veren's puzzlement. He didn't seem to understand where Charisse was going with the question and statement. But she did—Charisse was using the age gap between Veren and her as a weapon. It sparked her temper and incinerated her natural inclination to be prudent.

"Are we comparing manufacturing dates? Measuring shelf life? Or counting down to our best before?" Anza questioned.

All eyes swivelled in her direction, their expressions of surprise identical.

Except for Veren—amusement danced in his eyes. A slight warning entered it when she roused herself. With hands linked, she stretched them overhead, pulling on the muscles of her back. The hard rock and the cold air made it sore.

"We were discussing birth dates ..." Charisse's tone sounded defensive, and a touch antagonistic.

"Were you?" she asked sarcastically, not caring if she offended the woman.

"Was that a good cat nap?" Diego asked in a pacifying manner. The smile on his face seemed genuine.

"Yes, it was ... stimulating," she replied, smiling back. Of the three, Diego was the only one she liked. Marginally.

"Was there enough time for a dream?" Diego appeared to be bent on easing the tension that had built up between her and

Charisse. He was a peacemaker, a true gentleman. Anza appreciated it.

"Alas, no," she replied.

"Would you like to stretch your legs?" Diego had stood up, offering her his hand. She hesitated. Her muscles were tight, but she didn't want to leave Charisse to monopolise Veren.

Charlie got up, too. "That's a good idea, Diego." He faced Veren and said, "With your permission, Veren, can we accompany Anza for a walk?"

Veren looked at her, waiting for her to decide.

"Let them go, Veren. My cousin and Charlie are harmless. They'll take care of Anza," Charisse said, touching Veren's knee again.

"Why don't we all stretch our legs?" Veren suggested, standing up and pulling Anza to her feet.

She didn't realise her butt had gotten numb from sitting for so long. She winced and gasped as the blood resumed its restricted flow through the veins at the back of her thighs.

Veren heard her. "Are you okay, little one?"

"Pins and needles," she said, trying to rub the sensation back on her rump. Veren grinned as he watched her. "I'm ready." She shook off her legs.

With her hand curved into Veren's arm, they walked toward the end of the ridge, their steps slow and meandering. Diego had situated himself beside her. Charisse, as Anza expected, had slid her own arm through Veren's other arm. Charlie, it seemed, had lapsed into silence, and walked a step behind them all.

She wished the three would leave them alone. She wanted to ask Veren some questions, specifically what he meant when he declared himself her keeper.

Was he just joking?

What does it mean?

Veren's patience was running thin. These three humans and their normal ways shouldn't have bothered him, but they did. He didn't like how Charisse treated Anza, or how Charlie insulted her. He was glad that Anza's reaction to a crushing comment made her hackles rise instead. Her first instinct was to fight.

But the most bothersome thing was that Diego got on Anza's good side. Veren didn't want to look too deep into why it displeased him, since Diego wasn't as obnoxious as the other two, and making friends would benefit Anza.

During her brief stint here in Basco, she would have a chance at every human experience to create enough memories to last her a lifetime—so, she wouldn't want to do this again. The most ideal situation was for her to make them while Veren was around to protect her. He could help her assess which ones she could trust, and which ones she should stay away from.

Anza's instinct with people was good, but her youth and perhaps her desire to make connections would make her vulnerable. And, if tonight was an example, she was attractive in every way a teenage girl could be. She would draw that kind of attention wherever she went, especially when she learn to use her feminine charms.

He wondered now if her father ever taught her how to defend herself. Most females of their kind, at least the *Vis* he knew, had some basic training. It was part of the drill.

Anza didn't look trained, her body slim and slight like a normal human teenager. She didn't strike him as athletic, either. Maybe it was the combination of her physique and innocent face that made him want to make sure she was safe, unharmed, unhurt.

Anza's chuckle drew him out of his own musings. She was

laughing at whatever joke Diego told her. The boy was getting more successful in drawing her out by the minute. It chafed at him, but he didn't react. He would let Anza enjoy herself. This was temporary since she wouldn't see Diego again after tonight.

"I think my cousin and your ward are getting along fine. Don't you?" Charisse's comment was pointed as she leaned closer to him.

He could smell the pheromones emanating from her, but her wish would remain unfulfilled. He wasn't into one-night stands, and his work ethic forbade playing while on a job. Unlike the other males of his kind, he wouldn't dally with female humans just because it was common practice. *Brevis Amorem* may be a habit to most *Viscerebus* males, but it was not his.

The *Tribunal's* rules may justify the indulgence for brief affairs, since they were expected to keep relationships with female humans brief and impersonal, but it was not something he liked to do. He wouldn't add more parentless children in this world. No child of his would be a *Vondenad* left to survive alone in this world.

Charisse tugged at his arm, prompting him to respond to her earlier question.

"Anza is a friendly girl," he said with a glance at Anza and Diego. Anza's hand was still hooked on his arm, even if her attention was on Diego. That made him feel connected to her still. On an unconscious level, it anchored her to him.

"My cousin likes her very much. Charlie does, too. But, since Anza seems to prefer Diego, Charlie has stepped back," Charisse observed.

"We'll see. In the meantime, Diego had better behave himself. Anza is under my care." He said it loud enough for everyone to hear. It was a warning that he wanted Charisse to know, and for Diego to heed.

Anza and Diego stopped at the edge of the ridge and looked at him. Then, Anza pulled off the tablecloth draped around her shoulders and laid it on the grass. Charisse was quick to sit at Anza's right side after Anza took the first seat. With Diego at her left, they sandwiched Anza between them. Charisse's intention was obvious: the vacant space beside her was for Veren.

Veren opted to be behind Anza. An exasperated Charlie sat beside him.

Undeterred, Charisse twisted around to face him instead. Her disinterest in the incoming sunrise was made clear. Veren sighed, finding her persistence tiresome, although he couldn't help but be impressed by her extreme self-confidence—she ignored all the signals he was giving her. She seemed like a woman unused to getting rejected. Either that, or her manner of succeeding with them was by railroading their objections.

"So, Veren, do you have a girlfriend?" Her forwardness wasn't unexpected.

"No, I don't have a girlfriend."

Anza overheard his response and twisted to look at him. He placed his hands on her shoulders and made her face forward with a light pressure on her shoulder blades to keep her there. He rubbed gentle circles to reassure her.

Of what, he wasn't sure.

"What traits do you find attractive in a woman?" Charisse asked in a tone so saccharine, it was cloying. All her affectations were so unnatural—it was off-putting.

His response was a gentle shake of his head and a smile. Charisse pouted, unable to hide her irritation at his evasion.

Rays of sunshine started peeking out from the horizon, lightening the dark sky. The midnight blue hues transitioned to red violet. They were all transfixed at the sight. A welcome spate of silence enveloped them. Veren dug out his mobile phone and gave it to Anza, handing it to her from over her shoulder without an exchange of words. She glanced back at him with a grateful smile.

Another blast of cold air swept through them, making Anza shiver. Without a word, he grasped Anza's waist and pulled her back to him, close to his chest. His bent legs served as her armrests. She leaned back on him. His body protected her from the wind, warming her. Her silent sigh of contentment echoed his.

His chin rested at the top of her head, her back flat on his chest. They watched the sunrise on the horizon in complete silence. Anza held his mobile phone, her elbows propped on his knees. His arm hung loosely around her middle.

As the half globe of the sun showed, Anza aimed the camera at the view, watching the sun through the screen. The colours of the horizon transitioned from varying shades of violets to reds and yellows. Her eyes focused on the display, her fingers clicking at a furious pace.

"Two more minutes, Anza. You have enough beautiful shots," he whispered in her ear. A puzzled frown formed on her face as she glanced at him.

"Why?" Her question came a breath away from his cheek.

"So you can experience the sunrise—the photos can never capture that," he replied. "Be present, little one."

She nodded and lowered his cell phone. And for the succeeding minutes, they watched the sunrise until the whole globe of it emerged. The rays of yellow radiated from the centre sphere and painted the surrounding areas, layering them with red and orange.

It was breathtaking.

Anza took a deep breath and released it in gradual degrees. He felt her smile on his cheek, which triggered a smile of his own. "Shall we go?" she whispered.

"Yes. Let's get some breakfast along the way," he said. With a swift motion, he got up, pulling her too to her feet.

The rest of the group got up with them. Anza seemed surprised at their presence. He couldn't blame her. The complete silence and their shared moment earlier made him forget them, too. That wasn't a good thing if he was to become a great *Iztari*. Losing awareness of the surroundings could be deadly to a warrior.

"Are you guys leaving?" Charisse asked, stepping off the cloth as Anza tugged at it.

"We have to be on our way," Veren said. He took the cloth from Anza and folded it.

"Where are you off to next?" Diego's question was directed at him, but his eyes shifted to Anza.

She shrugged. Anza was waiting for him to speak for them.

"We'll decide along the way," he replied. He understood that Anza was as eager to leave their company as he was.

"Can we tag along?" Charisse asked.

He saw the spark of temper in Anza's eyes. She was close to saying something rude. He squeezed her fingers to stop her.

"We have a few things we need to accomplish. So, goodbye to you now. It's been a pleasure." He held out his hand to Charisse. She looked at it, unwilling to accept his handshake of farewell. Charlie grasped it instead.

"The pleasure was ours. Thank you, too," Charlie shook his hand. "Guys, I believe we have to get going, too. We've imposed our presence on them long enough. We don't want to take up more of their time."

Veren's dislike towards the guy lessened. It seemed he wasn't *that* self-absorbed.

Diego offered his hand to Anza, saying, "It was great meeting you and spending time with you, Anza."

She shook his hand and replied with a benign smile, "Likewise."

"Can I ask for your number? Maybe we can get in touch when we get back to civilization?" Diego's gaze and crooked grin seemed hopeful.

Anza hesitated.

"Anza doesn't have her phone right now. Give me your number and she can get it from me later," he said.

Diego hesitated for a moment, but dictated his number anyway. As he saved it on his phone, he wasn't sure if he could be selfless enough to give Diego's number to Anza after. He could only hope that Anza would forget to ask for it later.

"Can I have yours, Veren?" Charisse asked, her phone at the ready.

He gave her his number without hesitation. It was a burner phone, with a burner SIM card. Training protocol required that they destroy the phone and the SIM card after every case.

The three walked them to their bike. Just before Anza got on the bike behind him, Diego stopped her. "Call me, Anza, okay? I'd like to get to know you better as a... um... friend," he said. His hand clasped hers once more.

The warrior in him didn't like the feeling that bloomed in his chest at the sight of Anza's smile. It made him impatient to leave. The feeling faded as they zoomed out of the parking lot and onto the road, away from Diego, Charlie, and the persistent Charisse.

Veren stopped at a roadside eatery half an hour later. On the menu were fried rice, eggs with fried flying fish and the crispy, dried pork dish they had the night before. The meal came with dark coffee and brown sugar. It was served outdoors—the weather was perfect for it.

As they set the plates down, Anza's mouth watered at the aroma of hot, garlic fried rice. Intrigued, she watched Veren pour a quarter of his coffee on the rice. Veren laughed at her expression.

"You should try it. It's fantastic. I learned this from the Batangueños. They all pour coffee on their fried rice." With an excited lift of his eyebrow, he tucked into his food with enjoyment.

She copied him with more caution. She spooned some of her coffee over a bit of rice. Combined with the egg and flying fish, she had to agree with Veren. The smokiness of the coffee complimented the flavours and neutralised whatever oiliness there was in the fried rice and egg.

"That was delicious!" she said as the first mouthful assaulted her taste buds.

It was such a simple variation of a commonplace dish. Just a tweak. And yet, it brought her a new understanding of it, a new appreciation that made it more enjoyable.

"That's what travelling does to you. It enables you to experience other cultures. And the best way to do that is through their food," Veren said. "Have you travelled outside of the country before?"

"Yes, every year, with my parents." Somehow, her trips with her parents didn't have the feel of a novel experience or an awakening. With them, it was conventional, like a continuation of a routine, just in a different location.

He frowned at her lacklustre response. "Did that not make you perceive the people and their cultures in a different light?"

"It's hard to learn more about people when you encounter them at a distance, or to appreciate something new if your parents restrict you the whole time." She sighed. "It doesn't matter where we go, which attraction we visit, which restaurant we eat in: I feel like I still view my world through the narrow lens my parents set me up for."

Veren's intent gaze revealed his contemplation, as if her viewpoint was something he hadn't considered.

"I think we view the world through a narrow lens of our own experience," he stated, "and for most of us, each lens is different, but the size of that lens is within our individual control. Yours is a distinct case, I've got to admit."

They ate in silence for a minute or two as she weighed whether she would raise her next question now or later. Her impatience won.

"Veren, why did you say you were my keeper?" She had been itching to ask him the question since she first heard him say it.

Veren chewed, slow and prolonged. It appeared deliberate, as if he was buying his time to think of a decent response. "Well, that's the role I see myself having in your life..." It was a very casual response; it was almost evasive.

"What does it mean ... to be my keeper?" That he saw it as a role in her life implied permanence. Considering the limited time they had together, the statement confused her.

"Like a bodyguard, I guess. A mentor, a guidance counsellor, a friend ..."

"All of those require a constant presence." She had to point that out. When he left Basco, she would still be here. *How could he be my keeper if he's somewhere else?*

Veren stared at her. There was a line of strain around his mouth, as if he was in pain. It disappeared when he smiled at her, yet there was a touch of sadness to it.

"That's true, but with technology, there's really no way to lose contact with anyone you care about," he said.

A stab of sadness hit her. Once he leaves here, there would

be no way they could keep in contact with each other. For as long as she was hiding from her parents, she couldn't turn on her phone. She planned to hide for a year. She doubted that Veren would still remember her.

"For some people, yes. In my case, that wouldn't be possible," she said.

Veren's frown deepened. "Why? Don't you want to be friends with me?"

"While I'm in hiding, I *cannot* turn my phone on. That means I won't be able to text you, either." Even if she went back home, her parents would never allow her to form a relationship with a human like him.

"What about when you return home? Can't we keep in contact then?"

"No. My parents would never let me be friends with any human ... being." In the *Vis* world, she would go back to her isolated life. She didn't want to go back to that.

Veren was quiet once again. He turned contemplative, then took a deep breath and continued eating. When she didn't do the same, he prodded her. "Eat up, little one. Your food is getting cold."

She complied, but she had lost her appetite. There was no resolution, but it was no use forcing him to respond if he didn't want to. She had heard and witnessed his evasive moves last night. He was skilled at it.

Ten minutes later, as they were preparing for the ride back, a thought came to her: "If you are my keeper, does it mean that I'm your keeper in return?"

Veren paused from fixing her helmet. "When I'm ready to have a keeper, you'll be my first choice," he replied. "There you go—all done." He avoided her gaze and turned to straddle the bike.

She had no choice but to follow his lead. She got behind

him, like before, with her arms around his waist, her thumbs hooked inside his belt loops. But this time, while it was the most natural thing to do yesterday, today it felt awkward.

Just before he put his own helmet on, Veren looked back at her and said, "Little one, you need to hold on to me a little tighter. You've had no sleep and I don't want you to fall off during the ride."

"Okay." She leaned closer to him, her stomach pressed to his lower back, arms firm around his midriff, hands crossed and thumbs hooked on his belt loops. Her action became automatic; the awkwardness faded with his command.

Veren strapped on his helmet and away they zoomed along the picturesque country road. Like yesterday, they zigged and zagged past the stone, earthen and wooden homes; the mixture of blue sea and sky, the lush green of the hills, and the local people going about their daily chores.

She was content—something fundamental to her well-being settled in her heart. The hum of the motorcycle hypnotised her, and her last conscious thought was the hope that she could smell him through the helmet. His scent reminded her of home.

The silence and the stillness woke her up. Disoriented, she realised they had arrived back at the inn. She was still pressed along Veren's back, and his left arm was pressed on her right, left hand clasping her elbow.

Veren straightened when she moved. His hand loosened, but he didn't remove it, anchoring her to him still.

"You awake now, little one?" He asked over his shoulder.

"Yeah—Sorry. You were right. I needed the sleep ..." She straightened up. Her legs were wooden. She gasped when the rush of returning sensation attacked her limbs. Veren looked back at her in alarm. "Pins and needles," she muttered.

"Don't move," Veren said.

He manoeuvred his long legs off the bike, removed his helmet and then hers. The strap had left a mark on her chin, and Veren massaged it away. He then grasped her by the waist, lifted her, and set her gently on her feet.

She winced as the painful sensation of recirculating blood flowed to her veins, making her hop on each foot. Veren's hands remained on her waist, steadying her. Soon the prickles faded, allowing her to stand on her own. Veren's gentle fingers combed through her hair, ruffling it.

By instinct, she touched his hand, but before she could ask him what he was doing, he said, "Helmet head," and his hands dropped away.

"Thanks." Her hair must have looked like a bird's nest. "I think it's time to hit the shower. I'm starting to stink..." She needed a brief respite from her rioting emotions. Her resolution to treat him like an older brother was melting like ice cream in the midday sun.

"Yeah, me too. It's a wonder you were able to fall asleep on me like that. You must think I smelled like hell and the devil's ass combined." He ruffled his own helmet-flattened hair.

"No, the helmet was on the way," she blurted.

Veren laughed. She felt her cheeks heat up.

"Okay, so that redeemed this helmet from its hair flattening flaw." He chuckled.

"I guess," she said. "Are we going somewhere else later?" she asked to divert him from the reddening of her face and neck.

It was mid-afternoon. There was still the rest of the day, and Veren might have other plans for them. She needed re-energising. She felt lethargic.

"None for the day, but I'll meet you here later at six. Let's go out to dinner," he said.

"All right, I'll see you later ..." She proceeded to her room. She had a ton of things to do and so little time.

Her clothes needed to be washed, or she would have nothing to wear tomorrow. She had worn her two t-shirts, and if she wore this pair of jeans one more time, it might grow its own culture. Perhaps she would have enough time to go to the town centre and get a dress. She could afford one if she didn't spend over five hundred pesos.

As she got into the bathroom, she realised she was still wearing Veren's long-sleeved shirt. She rushed into the shower for a quick rinse. She wanted enough time to wash the clothes, go out to buy a dress, and come back in time for dinner.

To save time, she washed her shirt, underclothes and Veren's shirt under the shower using the hand soap that was provided in the room. It took a while as the soap wasn't foamy or meant for washing clothes. But it was all she had. She hung them on the verandah of the room to ensure that they would dry by morning. She would return Veren's shirt clean.

With her wet hair combed into place, she rushed out. She needed to get to the town square as fast as she could. It would be a good fifteen-minute walk, and she had about three hours to get ready for dinner. She wanted to have as much time as possible to make herself presentable.

Veren jogged down the stairs, checking the piece of paper he had and the written instruction on it. The front desk staff had given him directions to the town centre's best shop. He wanted to get Anza her own jacket. As he got out of the lobby and turned left, he saw Anza up ahead, hurrying towards somewhere.

Where is she going?

He followed her.

She might get into trouble.

Three blocks on, Anza turned left to the main street. The shop he meant to visit loomed over the horizon. He had kept the one-block distance between him and Anza, but lessened it as he realised he might lose her inside.

She just entered a clothes outlet when he got to the entrance. Anza disappeared through the door. He stayed out of sight and watched through the windows as she flicked through the hangers in the clothes rack. The racks were shoulder-height, and he could see every expression that crossed her face. There was an impatient frown on her forehead.

She was looking at dresses.

He realised Anza was a dress-wearing kind of girl, even if he hadn't seen her wear anything but jeans and a T-shirt since he met her. He supposed that, when she came with her parents for their holiday in their log cabin up in the mountains, a dress would have been inappropriate.

Anza had picked up a beautiful light and flowy, grey sleeveless summer dress with a tank top bodice and soft pleats under the breast. It had a profusion of tiny red, yellow and blue flowers embroidered on the hem that looked like it spilt from a basket.

Her eyes sparkled as she held it against her to check the fit. It was in her size. Then Anza looked at the tag. Her face fell. With a sigh, she put it back on the rack and walked away, but she glanced back with longing at the dress one more time. In her characteristic grit, she squared her shoulders and continued on to the rack closest to the wall.

He watched her pick up a short, blue eyelet blouse and a

skirt set. She held it against herself and examined her reflection in the mirror. She asked for another colour. The saleslady informed her there were three choices—blue, yellow, and green, then came back with what looked like a sea-foam green pair. The lady pointed to the dressing room to her left. Anza walked over and disappeared inside.

I should let her shop in peace and not spy on her like this.

Yet, he was compelled to keep watching. But his vantage point was bad. He couldn't see her well from this location. He entered the shop and headed towards the male section, then navigated between the racks of clothes for women and children. The shop was crammed and dusty. Grimy, beige linoleum covered the floor. The place smelled of plastic, floor wax, and packaging. The men's section was a little further at the back, close to where various shoes were on display.

"Good afternoon, Sir. How can I help you?" An eager saleslady approached him.

"I want to browse first. Can I go around for a bit? I'll call you when I need you." When the saleslady didn't respond, he asked, "Is it all right?" while exerting his charm. The saleslady blushed, nodded, and left him.

He positioned himself among the hanging clothes. Not looking, but waiting with bated breath for Anza to come out. To his disappointment, she wasn't wearing the new dress when she got out. She smiled at the waiting service staff and confirmed that she would get the set.

After she paid, Anza walked out, but not before throwing one last longing glance at the grey dress she had looked at earlier. With a sigh, she left the shop.

With her gone, he bought what he came here for—something warm for Anza to wear. He found a blue hoodie with a zipper closure on the front. It was the thickest he could find. On impulse, he bought the dress that Anza liked.

Satisfied with his purchase, he tucked the shopping bag inside his jacket and got out of the store. He hurried back to their inn, and within minutes, from a distance, he spotted Anza going the same direction.

He remembered the blouse and skirt pair she bought and wondered if she would wear it at dinner.

An hour and a half later, he sat in the lobby, waiting for Anza to show up. He was looking forward to seeing her in her new purchase.

Ten minutes in, he wondered what was taking her so long. She was uncharacteristically late. He approached the counter to call her room, but no one answered.

She could be on her way down now. It's a pity that she's not using her cell phone.

After another ten minutes without her, he got worried. He knocked on her door. There was no answer. For a moment, he felt tempted to kick the door in. Instead, he got the lock picking set that he always carried with him. A remnant of his childhood and a reminder of his troubled past, of what he had escaped from, what he overcame.

Every time he looked at it, it made him grateful for what he had, where he was, what he had achieved and the people who helped him. Today, he was grateful for it for a practical reason.

Within a minute, the door opened. Anza was lying on one of the two beds in her room, curled on her side like a child. Asleep. He felt a quick rush of relief to find her safe, but he saw the flush on her cheeks and realised she was running a temperature. He approached her and touched her cheek. Her fever was high. Heat emanated from her body.

She had laid out the clothes she bought at the edge of the

other bed, and beside it were the jeans she wore earlier. She was wearing the same oversized T-shirt. *It must be the one she borrowed from her cousin.* It was a good thing, as it was long enough to cover her. She was lying on the top of the sheets, shivering.

He whipped the cover from the other bed and draped it over her. He was tucking her in when Anza woke up, disoriented. She looked confused when she saw his face. Her eyes darted around.

Alarmed, she rasped, "Am I late?" She tried to get up but swayed even in a seated position.

"You're fevered. We're not going anywhere, so you're not late for anything." He pressed her back to the bed with gentle force and tucked her in.

"Give me a few minutes' rest, then I'll be fine," she said weakly, her eyes already closing.

"Have you taken any medicines?" He prodded her.

She shook her head. Her body trembled.

He phoned the reception and asked for some fever medicine. He didn't carry any—something he must rectify in his first aid kit. While he waited, he lay down behind her and pulled her close, infusing her with his warmth to stop the tremors that wracked her body.

The doorbell rang. It was the front desk clerk, with two paracetamol tablets in hand.

"Sir, these are the only two tablets we have. Do you need more?" the clerk asked.

"Yes, please," he said, giving a nod. "Can someone buy them for us?" He didn't want to leave her. The clerk nodded. "Is there a doctor on the island, just in case?" He didn't want to think about it, but it was best to be prepared.

"Yes, Sir. Should we call him?" The clerk peeked over his shoulder to ogle Anza.

Veren moved to block his view. He felt protective, and ... possessive.

"Not yet. Let's see first if the medicine works. If we need to call him, how soon can he come?" He wanted to plan, to prepare.

"If he's not at another house call, around ten minutes. His home clinic isn't very far from here."

"Okay. Thank you very much." He dismissed the clerk. Anza needed the paracetamol in her system as soon as possible.

He lifted Anza's upper body and slid behind her, leaning her back on his chest. Her body was scorching.

Holy Prometheus, she's on fire! This medicine better work.

He roused Anza with a gentle shake. She blinked up at him, her lids heavy. "Take this, Anza. It's for your fever."

He pushed the tablets through her lips. She complied, but it seemed to have taken most of her strength. She could barely swallow the tablets and the gulp of water.

He kept her pressed close to his chest until her shivering subsided. But her fever was still raging. He eased out from behind her. His body heat was adding to her temperature. She needed to cool down.

He realised she had unplugged the air conditioner in her room. No doubt—she didn't want to use it to save money. He turned it on to full blast, hoping it would help cool her down. He toed off his shoes and sat on the other bed, to stand guard and watch over her.

This was how it was to be someone's keeper—to be in charge of their physical, mental, and emotional welfare. It was such an enormous responsibility; he was unsure if he wanted it, but at that moment he had no choice. And, if he was honest with himself, he would have no one else care for her but himself.

For half an hour, he waited for the medicine to take effect, to control her fever.

Anza twisted in a sudden movement and flung the covers off. A long moan came out of her mouth. Fear struck his heart. He tried to rouse her, but she was insensible. She was close to convulsing. He picked her up and hoisted her over his shoulder to keep one hand free.

He went to her bathroom, turned the shower on and tested the water. She was burning up to a dangerous level, but the water couldn't be ice cold, just a few degrees cooler than her core temperature. He let her slide down his body until she was on her toes and anchored against him, his arm around her to support her limp body.

Heedless of his own clothes, he stood with her under the shower. The water flowed over both of them for a few minutes. One big hand held her head by the neck, so the cooling liquid could cascade from her crown to her feet without getting into her ears.

The water drenched them both, clothes and all. But it worked—Anza's fever abated, although she remained unconscious throughout. He reached behind her and turned off the shower. Still clasped against his chest to keep her upright, he pushed the hair off of her face. Anza stirred and briefly opened her eyes.

"Veren," she mumbled, then fell back into unconsciousness.

He walked her out of the stall where her towel hung. Beside it was the bathrobe provided by the inn. He took both. He wrapped the beach towel around her, and laid her on the bed. Her feet dangled over the edge. He knew he would have to get her out of her wet shirt. While he was concerned about her sensibilities, right now it was more important to keep her dry.

Without a second thought, he took the damp towel from her body, revealing the soaked T-shirt that was almost transparent. With his eyes averted, and with quick movements, he pulled the shirt off of her, and her underclothes followed. Her wet clothes landed on the floor with a splat. With determination, he pushed away every thought that had nothing to do with Anza's welfare and covered her with the dry bathrobe.

He didn't realise he held his breath while undressing her with averted eyes until he had to inhale. The air conditioner was blowing fiercely at him and sent shivers up his frame. He also needed to get out of his own sodden clothes. He peeled them off and pulled on the second bathrobe that was hanging in the wardrobe. It was thin, but it would do.

He collected their soggy clothes and dropped both sets on the bathroom floor. He towelled Anza's hair dry and ran her comb through the wet tresses. Tangled hair would greet her in the morning, and he was sure she wouldn't like that.

He fit her properly into the bathrobe, lifted, and placed her back on her bed. He pulled the covers over her and spread her damp hair on the pillow. She still had a mild fever, but her temperature was under control.

Thank Prometheus for that!

He was on his way to her bathroom to take care of their wet clothes when the doorbell rang. It was Mrs. Bassig, and she looked scandalised when she saw him in a bathrobe.

"Please, don't jump to conclusions, Mrs. Bassig." He stepped aside to let her in.

Mrs. Bassig walked in, speechless. She looked at him from head to toe, the raised eyebrows laden with questions and judgmental thoughts she dared not voice out for fear of having it confirmed.

"No doubt you came here because you heard Anza is sick." He glanced at Anza, still deep in slumber on the bed. "Her fever spiked so high, she was a second away from convulsion. I had to put her under the shower to lower her temperature."

Mrs. Bassig continued to stare at him. He could tell that she was trying to curb her own initial assumption. The older woman's considerable bosom heaved.

"Mr. Albareda, as far as I know, you just met Anza the other day in my lobby. Why are you suddenly so close to each other? What are your intentions towards this little girl?"

Mrs. Bassig's questions were direct. His impression was that she would not swallow a lie, and nothing would get past her sharp eyes and instinct.

"Mrs. Bassig, my intentions are pure. I assure you, I have done nothing, nor will I do anything that would harm her. All I want is to protect her and keep her safe." He infused his truth with as much sincerity as he could.

"But why are you doing this? What are you to her?" Mrs. Bassig asked.

"I'm her keeper." His reply was quick, automatic.

He could utter no truer words at the moment. And no one could make him unsay it.

Not Mrs. Bassig. Not even Anza's father.

7 THE REVELATION

"Who are you, really, Mr. Albareda?"

Mrs. Bassig's tone told him she wouldn't leave the issue alone until he answered all her questions to her satisfaction. At his hesitation, Mrs. Bassig's hands went to her hips. She bristled with authority.

"And don't tell me you're her keeper. *I* can take care of our young patient. She's staying in *my* inn. *I* have offered her employment, she's more *my* responsibility than yours."

Alarm streaked through him at her words. She threatened to cut his access to Anza if he didn't tell her the truth of who he was, why he was here, and what his connection to Anza was. He needed to tell her an acceptable variance of the truth.

He sighed. "Okay, Mrs. Bassig. You win ..." He sat down so he was at eye level with her. "My name is Veren Albareda. Anza's father, Manuu Soledad, sent me to find her, watch over her, and convince her to go home."

"Her father sent you?" Mrs. Bassig raised a disbelieving eyebrow. "How come she doesn't know you? She told me she met you here when you first checked in." Her tone sounded thick with suspicion.

"Because we have never met before." He glanced at the bed to check if Anza was still asleep. He didn't want her to overhear anything.

"Why send you? Are you a private investigator? You look too young to be one," Mrs. Bassig questioned.

"Do you mind if we move outside to talk? I don't want to disturb Anza." he said.

Mrs. Bassig gave his attire a pointed look. He shrugged. His clothes were wet, and he couldn't care less if people saw him buck naked.

After some hesitation, Mrs. Bassig nodded and opened the front door. He followed, barefoot and in a bathrobe. They stood in the hallway.

"Anza's father is a friend of my ... family. I just graduated from the military academy. I've been away for my studies. That's why Anza and I never met. Her dad asked me to convince her to come home. They didn't want to send anyone they don't trust."

He didn't create that brief explanation on the spot. It was part of his training to cover all kinds of situations. He had thought about this scenario before, except in his head, he was saying this practised statement to Anza.

"I gather Anza doesn't know yet who you are, and you don't want her to know..." Mrs. Bassig guessed correctly. Her objection to his strategy was plain in her voice. "So, what *is* your plan?"

"I want to ensure her safety while she's here and convince her of the merits of going home. She'd be more receptive to a neutral viewpoint. If she finds out who I am, that I'm part of the family, she'll put a wall between us. She'll dig her heels in, out of stubbornness." The reasoning was sound, and true. That had always been their concern about Anza.

Mrs. Bassig's indecisive stance softened. He could see that his explanation made sense to her. Finally, she nodded and said, "Okay. I'll keep your secret. But you can't take care of her dressed like ... that." She gestured to the bathrobe; her own thoughts had scandalised her.

"I was going to hang my clothes to dry and put them back on later. This was the only thing I could use for the moment. I wasn't planning to walk around your establishment wearing this robe. I just need this for the meantime."

"Give me your clothes and I'll have someone run it in the dryer."

Mrs. Bassig shooed him into the bathroom to get the wet clothes. He scooped them out into the damp towel and handed the entire load to her. Arms full of sodden clothing, she called something out over her shoulder, then added, "I'll send up some hot soup in an hour ... or so."

"Thank you, Mrs. Bassig."

He closed the door.

Anza was still deep in sleep. He touched her forehead. Not bad. He sighed and sat down on the bed, his back against the headboard. He wondered what caused the sudden onslaught of fever. The high temperature was the body's response to an infection. Hopefully, it was just a minor one.

His stomach rumbled. He was hungry. They both missed lunch earlier. He also wanted to get a spare change of clothes from his room, but the need to keep Anza in sight, not to leave her alone, was stronger. He would have to be in this bathrobe until Mrs. Bassig returned with his dry clothes. Maybe Anza would sleep on until then. He didn't want her scandalised like Mrs. Bassig.

Now that their innkeeper knew about him, the deadline to

accomplish his mission and tell Anza about himself loomed nearer. While Mrs. Bassig promised to keep his secret, she might make a mistake and slip up with Anza. He didn't want her to find out from someone else.

And to ensure her safety, he would make a bargain with Anza's father. To prepare her for the eventual life that she would live outside of her family, Manuu Soledad *must* give her more freedom. He must allow her to meet new people, to make friends, have a boy—experience life outside of her family, even in short bursts.

The thought of Anza being exposed to other people, other men in his absence, disturbed him.

———

Anza woke up just when the soup arrived, together with the food Veren had ordered for himself. She seemed confused, wanting to get up for whatever reason. He pressed her back on the bed with gentle and persistent force until she calmed down, her eyes focused on him.

"Are you hungry, little one?" he murmured.

She blinked up at him, glanced at the soup tray, and swallowed.

He smiled. "I'll take that as a yes."

He propped her up and spooned some into her mouth after blowing on it. She ate little, but the soup's saltiness made her drink a lot of water. He suspected Mrs. Bassig designed it so.

She was breathless afterwards, and dropped back to sleep like a tired child. He took the opportunity to eat. He had a hunch it would be a long night for him.

It was a good thing her room had two beds. He wouldn't have to suffer the small sofa or the floor.

Hours later, Anza kicked off her covers and shifted in her sleep. Her violent movement woke him up. He approached her bed to take her temperature. Her skin was clammy. She was drenched in sweat, her hair stuck to her forehead and neck, her pillow damp. She was on her side; the lamplight showed that the back of her bathrobe was wet.

He would have to change her into dry clothes. Since he would have to re-dress her with his eyes closed, his discarded bathrobe would be the easiest thing to change her into. With a sigh, he sat her up, her damp back supported by his chest. He kept his eyes focused on the ceiling as he peeled the bathrobe off her shoulders, one arm around her upper chest, his fist closed. He was careful not to touch her anywhere else. But glimpses of her creamy skin flashed in his line of vision.

With his free hand, he pushed the damp robe down, and pulled the other bathrobe over her naked back. He pulled her arms through each sleeve and wrapped the front of the robe around her, securing it. She had better be well-covered if she was going to keep kicking the bed sheets off.

That done, he pulled the damp robe from her and dropped it on the floor. He discovered her entire bed was almost soaked. She must have tossed and turned for hours. He put her on the other side of his bed, then whipped off the damp cover sheet from her bed to let it dry.

He took his place beside her and smoothed the hair off her face, spreading it on the pillow. Feelings of tenderness suffused him as he looked at her. This slight slip of a girl, with her innocence, grit, and fighting spirit, had penetrated his defensive wall. She was like a kitten, wide-eyed and soft. One couldn't help but melt inside while looking at her.

For now, she was his kitten. One he needed to take care of. Anza shifted and turned towards him, then huddled to his side. Her damp hair rested on his arm. He dared not pull her close—his body heat might increase her temperature again. So, he closed his eyes to savour the inner connection, this tenuous strand of understanding that had developed between Anza and himself.

It was precious, beautiful, fragile, and daunting.

"Veren ..."

A gentle prod on his side woke him up. Anza's sleepy gaze was on him as he opened his eyes. He was on his side, one arm slung over Anza's waist. He must have moved last night, as Anza's position was the same before he fell asleep.

"How are you?" His voice came out in a whisper. He pushed himself on his elbows and looked down at her.

"My throat hurts. I'm thirsty," she replied, her voice raspy. Her hand touched her own neck.

He stood up and got her a chilled bottle of water from the refrigerator. He helped her sit up, and she drank it fast. It drew a long exhale of relief from her. The hands that handed the bottle back to him trembled. Her breathing was short and quick, as if the action sapped all her remaining strength.

"Better?" he asked. At her nod, he touched her cheeks and forehead. She was cool to the touch.

"You need to eat—you're weak." He grasped her hand as it shook when she tried to reach for the bottled water again.

"I'm not hungry. I'm just thirsty," she said shakily.

"No, let's give you something easy to eat." He called the front desk to order some Arroz Caldo, a chicken and rice porridge for her, and some bacon and eggs for himself.

"Did you watch over me the entire night?" Her voice came out soft, her expression one of curiosity and concern.

"Yes, little one, I did." He nodded as he sat on the other bed. "I came looking for you when you didn't show up and found you asleep, and burning hot. Don't you remember?"

"No." Anza was trying to dredge her memory, but it must have come up blank. "The only thing I remember is taking a nap."

He pushed the limp hair off her pale face and pressed the cool, damp towel on her forehead, cheeks, and neck. Her eyes closed in bliss.

"Do you have any injuries? You might have an infection," She frowned in confusion at his question. "I'm trying to find out the source of your fever," he explained.

"No injury, but ...... my throat is sore," she replied, and swallowed. "It feels swollen, too."

He tipped her face up by the chin. "Say ahh."

She opened her mouth wide as he peered down her throat. Her tonsils were red and inflamed.

"Okay. Let's see if the swelling goes down within the day." It didn't look too bad. He was relieved. The island wasn't equipped for serious medical cases.

"Veren ..." she called as he stood up to go to the bathroom.

He looked back and waited for the rest of her statement. "Yes, little one?" he prompted.

"You don't have to pay for my fee, since I can't accompany you on your trip today," she said.

"Oh, don't be silly. You're keeping me company."

"No, you're nursing me. There's no need to charge you for the privilege," she said. Her attempt at humour made him smile. She was on her way to recovery.

"Let's discuss that later, little one—when you're strong enough to argue with me."

There was a knock on the door. Their food had arrived. He strode to the door and took the food tray in. "For now, you and I will eat."

Anza insisted on eating by herself. Despite her pronouncement on her disinterest in the food, she almost finished the porridge. This pleased him. As expected, she got sleepy after the meal. He was reading a book while Anza rested when his phone rang.

Edrigu was calling.

"Good morning, Sir." His mind debated with his heart whether to tell Edrigu about Anza being sick.

"How's everything, Veren? I'm due to call Manuu in half an hour, so I need an update from you," he said.

He understood Edrigu was asking not just for the truth of the status of his mission, but he also wanted a plausible statement they could give to Manuu.

He stepped out of Anza's room for privacy. "I have established a rapport, Sir. But I'm not yet confident that I can influence her enough to make her change her mind."

This was an accurate statement. Anza's reason for leaving was rooted deep, and he didn't think he would have enough influence on her decision.

"Is there anything you need to hasten the process? Manuu is worried and restless," Edrigu said.

"Yes, I think there is. I think it might be the only thing that would convince Anza to return and ensure she won't run away again. I need a commitment from him, Sir." He needed Edrigu to champion his cause, Anza's cause, to ensure her safety.

"What kind of commitment?" Edrigu sounded intrigued.

"He needs to promise to allow Anza to make friends with humans, to establish long-term friendships and ... relationships," he said. There was silence on the other line. "Sir?" he prompted.

"Is that what Anza wants?" Edrigu asked.

"Yes, Sir," he sighed. "She feels out of place in her own family, being the only Erdia among them. She can't take part in any of the things they do as *Vis*. Even so, her father treats her like a *Vis*. They all do."

He had to sway Edrigu to this cause. "She's not at all like us. She doesn't want to live her brief life unanchored, as our kind does. We have the longevity to do this, she does not. She does not want to waste her short lifespan living the *Vis* life when she doesn't have the years to sustain it."

"I see ..." Edrigu said.

Those two words carried so much understanding, it made his heart pound.

"Can you help me, Sir?" He heard the plea in his own voice. "I don't think Mr. Soledad will listen to someone like me, but he will with you."

"Veren, Anza is sixteen. In *Vis* years, she's practically a baby. She is his father's only child, daughter of his great love, the centre of his life. Therefore, he is understandably over-protective. While I see your point, a father's love is something we cannot question," Edrigu said, his tone gentle.

"Sir, it is the only thing that would convince her to come home, and stay home. Without that promise, Anza might just run away again. I believe Mr. Soledad is due for *Transit* next year. Anza might just do it again then. And this time, she might get lucky enough to disappear completely. It's the only way to keep her safe." The desperation in his voice was obvious to his own ears.

"Okay, that's a good argument. I will do my best to persuade Manuu to give her that." Edrigu sounded convinced.

An enormous rush of gratitude flooded his heart. "Thank you, Sir!" He could breathe easier now. Anza would be safe when he'd return to his training. He could focus on the rest of his life goals and not worry about her while away.

"So, what update can I tell Manuu?" Edrigu asked.

"You can tell him I have covered leads in Naidi and Vayang, and I have not found her there. I'm going to Valugan next," he said. This was half true. Those were the locations that he intended to visit with Anza.

"Okay. That will work. I don't expect him to say yes immediately, but I will convince him of the merits of your plan," Edrigu said. "I'll call you in a day or so. Earlier if I succeed with Manuu on my first try."

Waves of confusing emotions washed over him when he realised that if Edrigu secured Manuu Soledad's commitment tomorrow, he could reveal himself to Anza and convince her to go home. And, if she agreed, perhaps in two days they would part ways.

My time with her would end.

I should be glad.

I should be happy that I'm so close to completing my mission.

Instead, he felt deflated.

Anza woke up in the dim lamplight.

Did I sleep all day?

She glanced at the other bed and saw Veren asleep, an opened book lying face down beside him. He looked peaceful and boyish.

This must be what he looked like before the troubles he took upon his shoulders weighed on him. At twenty-three, he struck her as more serious than he should be. Despite his lighthearted manner, there was something grave that underpinned his actions.

She stretched out and her tight muscles protested. She had been abed for far too long and needed a shower. It propelled her to go to the bathroom. After a short, cool rinse, she put on the same bathrobe she wore earlier. The feeling of cleanliness and the scent that lingered in the bathrobe gave her a sense of well-being. She sniffed at the robe, trying to remember where she had smelled it before.

She padded out to the verandah and sat on a cushioned rattan lounger. The cool sunset breeze soothed her. The fresh and fragrant scent of sea, jasmine, wet grass, and some unfamiliar vegetation perfumed the air. Day birds had changed shift with their nocturnal kin, their call now dominated the night air. The cricket chirps accompanied their song.

She sat curled up and hugged her knees close, enveloped by the comforting darkness. The first week of her journey for independence had been eventful. Fate seemed determined to show her, at first instance, what it would be like on her own. If Veren didn't show up, she would have been sick alone, in a bed space, with no one to help her.

Her life wasn't in danger, but if something direr had occurred, it would devastate her father. If he never ever found her, or her body, he would suffer for a long time not knowing what became of her. Her impulsive action to run away was irresponsible, and selfish. She knew that she needed to rectify it, that she must relieve her parents' anxiety about her health and safety.

The door behind her slid open with a thud, startling her. A frantic Veren followed. His eyes were wild and furious.

"What the hell, Anza!"

Veren loomed over her. His body vibrated with menacing

energy. She looked up at him, confused by the anger on his face.

"What did I do?"

"I woke up, and you were gone. You ... I looked all over for you ... I thought ..."

"I'm sorry, I wanted some air. I didn't realise you would worry ..."

He stood looking down at her for a while, fists clenched. He exhaled, and the tension bled out of him. With a sigh, he tapped her leg to make her scoot over so he would have room to sit down. She did. Veren dropped beside her.

"Why didn't you wake me?" His tone was calm. The light from the bedroom no longer illuminated his face, darkness hiding his expression from her.

"You were sleeping. You needed your rest too." She tucked her legs under herself to hide her toes. The night air had turned cold.

Veren scooped her into his lap. One hand covered her bare feet. The heat from it warmed her toes. She went rigid for a moment, but soon settled into him. She curled into his chest and laid her head at the curve of his neck. This felt right, being cradled in his arms. It was safety, comfort, affection all rolled into one warm cocoon.

Ahh. The smell is Veren. He wore this before I did.

This realisation made her heart hum. It still had that elusive whiff of something familiar yet unknown embedded in the robe, but she was too content at the moment to delve deeper into her memory bank.

"You scared me, little one," he murmured.

"I'm sorry. I didn't mean to." She inhaled deeply. With this breath, a decision solidified within her, borne out of the insight that came to her tonight. "I seem to have a habit of unintentionally scaring the people who care about me."

Veren's body tensed. She could sense his eyes on her.

"Did you come to an epiphany during your fever?" he asked.

That made her smile. "Not quite an epiphany. Just a realisation that I've been selfish. I didn't think about how much my father and my family would worry about me when I left like that."

"Wait—does this mean that you've changed your mind about your plan? To be independent and live away from them, I mean."

There was a hitch in his voice that she didn't quite understand, but she let it go.

"Not quite. I still want to achieve independence. But I need to amend my methods, so I won't worry my parents unnecessarily. I guess they still see me as a child."

"You can do it gradually, Anza. Not like this—not cold turkey."

"Right," she yawned. "Not cold turkey."

Veren felt Anza's weight settle on him as she fell asleep. The hand that rested on his chest slid down to her lap. Her breathing became an even cadence. She slept like a child—complete, trusting, vulnerable.

This had become a habit between them. Him watching over her slumber as she dreamed. He wouldn't have it any other way.

He took in a deep breath, then released it. Every molecule of air flushed away the remnants of the fear that had gripped him earlier when he thought she'd wandered off in a fever-induced sleep. He went on a frantic search for her in the hallways. And the stairs, half afraid that he might find her broken body at the bottom.

He was in the garden when he looked up and saw someone smoking on a verandah. He realised he didn't check the one in her room. The only thing that stopped him from climbing the verandahs from the front was the smoking guy. It would shock the man to see him scale the building one verandah after another. That could cause a ruckus.

He rushed back to her room. His relief when he found her curled on the small couch overwhelmed him. Then he got angry at himself for overreacting.

Anza had carved a space in his heart, a fact that he found alarming. She was too young for him, and he had no time for love in his life right now. Her impulsiveness, her drive for independence, required someone who would watch over her constantly while allowing her to grow.

He couldn't afford to be derailed. His path was set and the timetable for each milestone, fixed. This case was supposed to be a stepping stone, but she turned out to be a divergence from the direction he had chosen since childhood.

His frustrated sigh echoed her sleepy one. She shifted in his lap and straightened her legs. He looked down at her sleeping form and cradled her closer, rocking her. Holding her like this, entrusted in his keeping, somehow soothed his anxiety. It made him believe that life would sort itself out in the long run.

It gave him hope.

Their conversation earlier showed him the time to convince her to go home had come; she was ready for it. She had loosened her grip on her idea of independence. She was ready for a compromise.

He knew he could convince her to go home before the end of the day tomorrow if he applied himself. And they would be on her trip back home the day after. She would be with her father then, and he would be on his way. It would be 'Mission Accomplished' with a day to spare. His schedule would return to normal, but the rest of his life never would.

Anza sneezed. It alerted him to the dropping temperature and reminded him that she was still recovering. He stood up and carried her with ease back to the room, then laid her down on the bed, tucking her in.

He stood by her door as he fought the desire to stay. The knowledge that he had another day with her made him close the door and walk away.

If he must learn to let her go, he might as well start now.

Pangs of hunger woke Anza up. She was disappointed when she saw the empty bed next to hers. Veren must have decided last night that she didn't need to be watched anymore.

The sky was just lighting up now with the morning sun. She wondered if the kitchen was already open. Her stomach growled. She felt normal, but her hands trembled a little. *Must be my hunger*.

To revive herself, she took a full shower to wash away traces of her illness. She put on the sea-green eyelet dress she bought the other day. She was going to wear it the night she fell ill. Now that she felt better, she wanted to look good.

She got downstairs and found that the coffee shop had just opened for the day. The staff was turning on lights and setting tables. The kitchen wouldn't be ready for another hour. They offered her coffee while she waited. She accepted it and took it with her as she walked to the bakery located two blocks away. An hour was too long to wait. Also, she wanted fresh air—the walk would do her good.

A block in, she was out of breath and reconsidering the

wisdom of her decision. She rested and weighed the pros and cons of continuing to the bakery—she was halfway there already—or going back to wait for the kitchen to open.

She was gauging the distance between her two options when she saw Veren hurrying her way. His expression was thunderous. And she knew the reason for that look. She waited for him to come closer and as he loomed over her; she gave him her best heartfelt smile. It worked as intended. Veren faltered mid-step and forgot whatever he intended to say at the sight of her beaming face.

"Good morning, Veren. What brought you out this early?"

He blinked at her. Twice.

Resigned, he asked, "Why are you out this early, Anza?"

"I was hungry. I want to buy bread." She pointed to the bakery.

"You're not recovered enough yet to be walking this distance." He led her to a wooden bench at the corner of the street. "You wait here. I can get you what you want. Anything in particular?"

"I can go with you ..."

"No. You're already breathless. Just sit there, and I'll be back shortly."

He sounded like her father whenever he didn't want any argument or negotiation. It made her smile.

"So, what do you want?" Veren persisted.

"Some pandesal? Or anything with meat in it, like meat pies, or sandwich buns. Anything savoury ..." Veren's eyebrow raised in surprise. "I'm hungry," she said in her defence.

He reached out and touched her cheek, smiling. "That's a good sign. Your appetite is back. And your temperature is normal." With one last appraising perusal, he departed.

She watched him jog to the bakery. Her heart fluttered.

How exactly did Veren see her apart from as a little sister? His affection and concern for her warmed her soul.

The sound of jogging feet made her turn her head. It seemed there was another early riser today. To her surprise, she recognised him as Diego. He skidded to a stop in front of her, jaw going slack in surprise.

"Anza!" The delight in his face was clear.

"What are you doing here, Diego?"

"Jogging. We're staying four blocks away from here." He pointed in the bakery's direction. "I'm on my way back to our hotel."

"What a coincidence!"

"Where are you staying? And why are you here?" Diego's questions were tripping over each other.

"I was going to buy bread from the bakery. Veren is doing that for me."

"Oh ... So, he's still with you?" His frown seemed wary.

"Yes. He's my keeper, remember?"

"Yeah, I remember. Although, I still don't know what it means," Diego said, his tone inviting an explanation from her. He would be disappointed, as she had no inclination to do so—she didn't know how to define it herself.

In perfect timing, her keeper approached, a brown bag full of bread in his hand.

"Good morning, Diego. It's quite a coincidence to find you out and about this early in the morning." Veren's deep voice lacked much intonation, but still sounded thick with meaning.

"Good morning, Veren, and I agree. It's quite a pleasant shock to encounter Anza here. But it makes my day."

"It looks like you were out jogging, so we won't keep you. Anza needs to eat and rest for now." Veren may have been polite, but he was also dismissive. He grasped Anza's elbow, clearly intending to bring about her eating and rest as soon as possible.

The highhandedness annoyed her, but she had no energy to argue with Veren in the street, and certainly not in front of an audience. "Bye, Diego," she said in a cheerful voice as she waved at him. "It was nice to see you again."

Diego had no choice but to nod. His expression reflected his unvoiced protest.

She and Veren walked back to their hotel, bag of bread in hand. They settled on a chair set outside of the coffee shop. Veren took out the contents of his purchase. The smell of freshly baked bread made her mouth water.

A pandesal and a beef bun later, she was a new woman. The coffee was the perfect pair for the pieces of bread. Veren consumed the rest, and when the staff informed them that the kitchen was ready to take their order, he asked for scrambled eggs.

"You're still hungry after all that bread?" His appetite amazed her.

"I'm a growing boy," he joked. "Plus, the jog to the bakery sapped my energy."

"Oh, that reminds me ..." Her earlier annoyance at his domineering manner returned. "I dislike it when people decide for me."

His eyebrow raised. "Did you not need to eat and rest earlier? You braved the distance just to get something to eat, and you were breathless in the effort. That shows you were both hungry and tired."

"Yeah, but that's beside the point."

"Well, you can discuss your point when you're well and have enough breath to argue," Veren said, ending their discussion on that topic.

It was hard to sustain her annoyance when he had a valid argument. She would let it slide, for now.

Anza and Veren spent the morning by the garden under the shade of the trees, with Anza dozing off a few minutes at a time. But she was on the mend, and her recuperation satisfied him. He wanted her recovered for their talk about her homecoming.

The day was breezy; the garden was fragrant with jasmine, the sky blue and cloudless. His heart felt full of emotions as he watched her nap against him. Anza looked better in a dress. She looked less like a child in it than in jeans and oversized shirts. She was on the brink of blossoming into full womanhood. It pained him to think he wouldn't be there to watch it happen.

For now, he needed to finish his mission, to fulfil what he meant to do when he came looking for her; to convince her to come home.

The opportunity came over lunch. He had food delivered to her unit and set it all up on her verandah. He wanted the perfect ambience and privacy for their talk.

Anza ate well. She even had a hankering for dessert, so he ordered some fruits for her. Over her ginger tea and his coffee, he raised the question that was at the surface of his mind.

"Anza, last night you mentioned changing your plans to achieve independence. What changed?"

"I want my parents to know that I'm well," she said.

"How would you do that?"

"I'd like to borrow your phone for a start, so I can text them and tell them I'm okay." Her eyes held an appeal for him to say yes. "I plan to send them regular messages later, perhaps once a week, once I get a new phone."

140

"Anza, a text message once a week won't stop your father from worrying. Only one thing would do that. And you know what that is." He could relate to her father's anxiety. The thought of leaving her here alone and unprotected was knotting his gut into pretzels.

"I can't give up on my independence, Veren. It's crucial to my future ..." Her response carried defiance, desperation, and regret.

"You wouldn't have to give up on your quest. There's a better way to do this."

"How?"

"Negotiate with your dad. Tell him why you want to do this and then ask him to allow you to make friends and establish relationships with people outside of your family."

Anza digested his suggestion, determining the viability of it. "Do you think my dad would agree?" Hope glinted in her eyes.

"You're in a better position to answer that, Anza. I don't know your father ... as well as you do." He took a gulp of his coffee. "But, given his bitter experience this past week, he would know you're serious and that it's worth considering."

Anza went quiet for a while, chewing on the inside of her lower lip as she contemplated her circumstances and the options available to her.

"It might work ..." She nodded to herself, then sighed. "I wish I had asked him before I ran away."

"Well, look at it this way. The pain of the past week added weight in your favour to sway him to your cause."

She smiled. "You have a good point there."

"So, are you ready to go home tomorrow?" He wanted to bring her to her father himself, to ensure that his last image of Anza was that of her surrounded by the people who loved her.

"Yes, I am," she said with a nod. "How about you? When are you planning to leave here?"

"I was thinking that we can travel together; fly back to the mainland tomorrow."

"Why would you cut your visit here short?" She was perplexed.

"I want to make sure you get home safe and sound."

"Veren, I don't want you to cut your holiday short on my account."

"I can come back here anytime," he reassured her. "Besides, I need to go to the mainland tomorrow. There's something I need from there that I can't get here." He needed his *sustenance*, since his *vital hunger* was surfacing. He could feel his *Crux* weakening. The telltale tightening of his core had begun this morning.

"Are you sure?" She looked doubtful. "You're not just saying that because you're taking your role as my keeper seriously, are you?"

"No, I'm not saying that because I'm your keeper. However, I *do* take that role seriously." He pressed her mouth closed with his forefinger when she was poised to argue. "So, it's settled. We're flying out together tomorrow."

Anza looked unconvinced, her eyes narrowed as she seemed to be readying herself for an argument. And he remembered their last exchange. His chest tightened with the effort not to coddle her, like her father did.

"Anza, I am not deciding for you in this instance. I am choosing for me. And I really want to fly with you. Will you let me?"

She looked at him intently, then a slow smile appeared on her lips. She nodded. "Okay." She went back to eating her fruits.

Warm feelings invaded his heart as he watched her eat. He

wondered if he should tell her who he was, why he came here. It was an unnecessary barrier between them.

Will she be angry at me for deceiving her? Maybe I should warn her father not to divulge who I am to her.

"After lunch, why don't you go take a nap? I'll go to the airport and buy our tickets."

"Okay, but let me give you money for my fare." She jumped up to rush off.

He held her arm to stop her. "It's okay, little one—I can take care of it."

"I insist, Veren. Besides, I don't have to pinch pennies now. I'm going home." Her mouth had a stubborn curl to it.

"Okay." He let her go; the determined glint in her eyes brooked no argument.

Anza came back soon after and handed him the money.

"I should call my dad first. He could be in Manila," she said, thinking aloud.

"He won't be," he said on impulse.

Anza looked at him, surprised. "How would you know?"

"Well, um... if I was your father, I would stay where you left me, in case you return."

She paused and considered that. "I guess so."

He got up and kissed her forehead. "Bedtime for you, little one. I'll take care of our tickets."

On the way to the airport, he battled regret, sadness, gladness, hope, and some other emotion that he couldn't name. It was too alien for him to identify.

All he knew was that it stemmed from the reality that he was parting ways with Anza by tomorrow.

8 THE KEEPER, THE VISCEREBUS

The mixed feelings that ruled him as he completed his task weighed in his heart. He had secured the tickets. The inevitability of their parting was now tangible. He was both reluctant to hurry back and wanting to take his time. With the moments ticking by, he wanted to squeeze every second with Anza, and yet, not seeing her felt like he was holding back time.

As if Fate wanted to rub it in, his phone rang. It was Edrigu.

"Good afternoon, Sir," he said. Edrigu's call was another dose of reality.

"Good afternoon, Veren. How are you doing with your mission?"

"We're flying to the mainland tomorrow. Anza agreed to go home." His heart weighted down by that declaration.

"Congratulations. I knew you could do it." Edrigu's pride in him should have lifted his spirit, but it didn't. "Did she make a fuss?"

"No, Sir. She came to her own resolution when she got sick.

But the idea of negotiating a measure of freedom from her father convinced her, ultimately."

"Well, she won't have a hard time. Manuu agreed." Edrigu sounded smug.

That was welcome news, but that information was like the closing of a door.

"What did he agree to, Sir?"

"We didn't discuss the details. Just that he would allow Anza to make friends with humans, and keep in contact with them. I trust Anza can handle it herself. Based on your reports, she's got pluck."

"Yes, she's got that in buckets." He was proud of her. Anza would hold her own against her father.

"So, does she know who you are? Have you told her?"

"No, Sir. To her, I'm a friend she made here on the island. Her first human friend. A temporary keeper."

"A temporary keeper ... I see." A brief silence ensued. Edrigu seemed to have understood the pain in Veren's heart. "Should I expect you to be back here by tomorrow as well?"

"Yes, Sir, I booked a flight in the afternoon."

He had today and tomorrow with Anza, and he planned to make the most of it.

He was perusing the tourist brochure for a place to take Anza to dinner later that evening when someone tapped him on the shoulder.

"Hi, bro." Diego stood beside his table, uncertain yet defiant.

"Diego"—Veren stood up, surprised—"What brings you here?"

"I was looking for a place to eat, and ..." Veren's direct look made Diego falter. "Fine. I came here looking for Anza. I saw you guys go in here earlier."

"Why are you looking for Anza?" There was no use in prevaricating, in pretending he was unaware of Diego's interest in her.

"I'll be honest with you, Veren. I like Anza very much and I want to be her friend." Diego's straight reply and unwavering gaze impressed him. Most guys wouldn't challenge another male if they could help it.

"Diego, I can't stop you from pursuing her. Only Anza can, frankly." This truth was obvious to them both, but he knew Diego wanted to hear it from him.

"So, you won't stop me?"

Diego was asking for his permission, he realised. As much as Veren would have liked to deny Diego the pleasure, he didn't have it in him to impede what would be beneficial for Anza.

"Of course I won't, but you must accept the responsibility for what your actions would do to her. Anza's young—a sixteen year-old. She had a sheltered upbringing and she's naïve. If you take advantage of her, if you hurt her, you'll colour her view of life and men from then on." He paused only to take a breath. "So, are you prepared for that?"

He was daring Diego to give him his word, to prove to him that he was as honourable as he seemed to be. Diego stared at him, gauging his sincerity, it seemed.

"Yes. My intention is pure. And if friendship is the only thing she wants at the moment, I'll be a friend to her." Diego's statement conveyed that he wanted more.

Part of him wished Diego had backed down. Emotionally, Anza was a blank slate. If a human like Diego showed her kindness, she might just fall in love with him. Veren felt a twinge of fear. But he couldn't put his self-interest above Anza's. Her welfare was more important.

"What she wants and what she needs might not be the same thing." Veren couldn't help but stress the point again. "Are you committed to putting her needs above your own?"

If Anza was going to go out into the world, it would help that she had another human in her life who wouldn't take advantage of her lack of experience. Especially since he couldn't be with her, to watch out for her.

"I have never taken advantage of anyone in my life, Veren. I'm not about to start with Anza." Diego's defensive response was empathic, but not enough for him.

"Diego, Anza needs someone who would allow her to experience life. She needs to make many friends, to develop relationships that would expand her horizon. Would you allow her to grow into her own person before making her yours?"

Diego stood still for a long moment; his eyes never left him. The understanding that dawned on Diego's face chafed at Veren's insides. It made him feel raw and exposed.

"Is that what you're doing, Veren?"

Diego's question struck him with the force of a sledgehammer. His jaw tightened. He had to swallow to loosen the knot in his chest.

"Can you do it?" He asked, ignoring Diego's question.

Diego nodded and released a long in-drawn breath, then held out his hand—a man's offer of his commitment. Diego had just accepted to take his place in Anza's life as her keeper. Veren shook the other man's hand; it was the sealing of a pact, the passing of a baton.

And it was a blow to his heart.

"When can I see Anza?" Diego asked, clearing his throat.

"Not today. We're leaving Basco tomorrow." He wanted all of Anza's remaining hours here to be only his. Every single second.

At Diego's expression, he took a piece of paper and wrote

Anza's phone number down. "Here you go. Anza's number. Her phone is off at the moment, but she'll turn it on when she returns to Manila." He handed it to Diego. "I'll tell her to expect your call."

Diego looked at it and considered him, "Thank you, Veren." He pocketed the paper. Then, with a nod, he turned and left.

His borrowed time with Anza was bleeding away fast. With grim determination, Veren proceeded to where she was.

Anza was still napping in her room when he entered. He watched her for a while, memorising the curve of her shoulders, the relaxed, half-opened mouth, the lashes that threw a slight shadow on her baby-soft cheeks, and the gentle rise of her body as she slept. He would commit this to his memory, etch it in his heart. This child-woman that destiny threw in his path continued to create chaos in his soul without knowing it, and with so little effort.

He laid down the dress he bought for her a few days ago at the foot of the bed. He hoped to see it on her tonight.

It would be his one and only chance.

———

Mrs. Bassig allowed them to use her vehicle when she found out he was planning to take Anza to Fundación Pacita for dinner. She didn't want Anza exposed to the chilly night air, which she would be if they rode his rented motorbike.

When Anza showed up wearing the grey rayon dress, it rendered him speechless. She fixed her hair into relaxed waves, and she was wearing makeup. She gave him a glimpse of what she would be like as a woman, when she'd be old enough for him.

Emotions choked him up.

"You look stunning, little one," he said through a tight throat. His voice sounded rusty, even to his own ears.

"Thank you," Anza said, throwing him a bemused look. "And thank you for this dress. How did you know I wanted it?" The glitter in her eyes was challenging, and a tad suspicious.

He swallowed a kick of panic in his constricted chest. "I saw you look at it in the shop a few days ago."

One delicate eyebrow quirked with warning. "You were following me?"

"No. I was going to the same shop... to get you a hoodie, so you won't be cold when we travel." His pulse was rioting while he waited for Anza's response.

Her eyebrow lowered and erased the suspicion in her eyes. She smoothed the dressed down. Her smile was shy, and grateful. "Thank you, again."

"You're welcome." He gulped down his relief. "Shall we?"

She took his offered arm and walked with him to the waiting car.

"No bike tonight?" Anza asked, surprised. She looked around for the motorcycle.

He smiled at her. "No. Mrs. Bassig doesn't want you to get too exposed to the night air."

"Oh! Does that mean we're going somewhere far?" Her eyes were alight with excitement.

"Not far, but somewhere special," he replied, and ushered her to the passenger seat.

"Where are we going?"

"You'll like it. You'll see."

———

A garden glittering with hundreds of tiny fairy lights greeted them. Fundacion Pacita was perched atop rolling hills, with a three-hundred-sixty degrees of amazing view. The beautiful stone building made her think of a small castle ruling over a compact kingdom. It had an otherworldly ambience.

Veren booked a table for them on the verandah with the view and the sound of the wind-swept ocean. Their illumination came from the glass lamp set on one corner of the table. They sat side by side, allowing them to enjoy the scenery and talk at a comfortable level.

Few words were exchanged between them during dinner. Veren seemed content. He gave her smiles, affectionate little touches, and pleased looks. As for her, she was just happy being there with him, in this peaceful setting. Time was fleeting, and words seemed to make the clock move faster. Silence was the best way to savour the moment.

She recalled when she woke up earlier that day, thinking of the grey dress that she regretted not splurging on. It was like a miracle to find it there, draped at the foot of the bed. For a moment, she thought she dreamt it. It could only be Veren who got it for her. She thought it an odd coincidence that he picked up the one dress she really liked in the shop. But then, the shop was small, the choices weren't varied and the grey dress was the best among the selection.

It was not the most expensive dress she had ever owned. Not even close. But to her, this dress was invaluable. Veren gave it to her at the time she wanted it most. It made her look and feel like a woman, or at least older than her current age. And, with the aid of make-up, she felt worthy of the opportunity to breach the age gap between her and Veren tonight.

As she glanced his way, she caught him studying her, a look of indecision on his face. But he took a deep breath and his smile chased it away.

"Why were you looking at me like that?" She wanted to know what was on his mind, to see if she read him right.

"What do you mean?"

The flickering light of the lamp made it hard for Anza to read his thoughts as the shadows danced across his face.

"Earlier," she explained, "you looked like you were weighing your options, and whatever it was, you decided against it."

"I was weighing ... whether I was going to order dessert or not, but I had enough ... food already. It was just ... greed," he replied.

She sensed he wasn't referring to food, but she let it pass.

"What's our plan tomorrow? What time do we leave?" The thought of going home and seeing her father again gave her butterflies in the stomach.

"Eleven a.m. We need to leave the hotel by eight. Will you be ready by then?"

"Yes—all of my possessions fit in my backpack." Packing her bag had brought the finality of her decision home. "Where are you staying in the city?" She was compelled to ask him. She didn't want to cut their connection short.

"I don't know yet, but I can escort you to your home, to your father." He covered her hand in assurance.

"You don't have to. I can call him. He'll want to pick me up at the airport." She didn't want him to feel obligated.

"I want to do this, Anza."

Why? "As my keeper?"

"As your keeper."

"How long are you going to be one, Veren?" She leaned closer to read his expression better.

He paused before answering, "For as long as it takes."

It was still a vague, unsatisfactory response, but the promise of a future reassured her. If her father agreed to her bargain, Veren would be her first official human friend. And she couldn't have done better. Her father wouldn't fault her judgment on Veren.

An icy breeze swept over them, making her shiver. Veren took off his jacket and draped it over her shoulder, grasping the front of it close.

"Shall we go?" he asked, tapping the end of her nose.

She nodded.

As she stood by the entrance, Veren stopped. She glanced up at him, wondering why.

"I've got a request, little one." Veren smiled down at her, tucking the wisps of hair behind her ear.

"What is it?"

"Can I take a photo of you?" He held up his phone, crooked half-smile on his face.

She didn't expect that. *Veren wasn't the selfie-taking kind.*

Bemused, she nodded. With the fairy-lighted garden as a backdrop, Veren took a photo of her on his phone. The seriousness in his face as he took the shot made her smile—the satisfied glint in his eyes as he looked at his picture widened it.

On the leisurely drive back to their hotel, Veren stopped by every lookout point along the way and took more photos. It was like Veren was trying to capture all their moments together as much as he could, cram as much of it in the remaining time they had together, and record them all in his phone for posterity.

"You have to give me copies of those shots, Veren," Anza said in jest. It was her attempt to drive out the unsettling emotions from her heart.

"Of course. I can transfer them to your phone later. Have you turned it back on, by the way? Or called your father, for that matter?"

"No, not yet. I was planning to do it tomorrow when we're

at the airport." The thought of calling her father made her stomach ache.

Veren squeezed her hand. "Everything will be okay, little one."

Somehow, she believed him. His certainty gave her confidence.

They got back to the hotel just before the wind changed. The downpour that followed made their shared coffee on her verandah cosy and heart-warming. There was something soothing about being together while watching a storm rage outside. It made the turmoil in their hearts seem inconsequential.

They spent the late hours of the night and well into the early hours of the morning talking about life, anything, and everything. During the moments of silence, they were in accord. No conversation was necessary.

Veren held her close to him for hours. They remained awake and witnessed darkness turn into light. They listened to the whispering wind that turned into a howl as the morning came and the rain intensified. Flashes of lightning made the swaying streams of rain visible. Stormy weather had never looked as fascinating or compelling. Dark clouds hid the sun, giving them the illusion that night refused to give in to morning, that it was here to stay and prolong their remaining time together.

The moment was broken when Veren received a text message. His serene expression turned into alarm as he read it. His grim silence and the hardness in his expression unnerved her.

"What happened?"

"They cancelled our flight because of the poor weather." Veren's flat tone scared her. It seemed to have created a panic in him.

"It's not too bad ... isn't it? We can re-book tomorrow, or the next day ..." Her voice faltered as the dread in his eyes grew. He didn't seem to hear her. Her heart hammered violent beats against her chest.

"Anza, I have to go ... somewhere. I need to do something. Stay here. I'll be back later," Veren said, then rushed out of the door. He didn't wait for her response.

For the first time in her life, she was frightened. Of what, she didn't know. It was a premonition of something terrible, and it settled like a boulder in her stomach.

Veren phoned Edrigu multiple times, but the signal was bad. He sent him a text message, just in case. It was a disaster to be stranded here today. There was no *Tribunal* source of *victus* here in Basco. The population was too small. No morgue or hospital to steal fresh human heart, liver or kidney from.

His *vital hunger* was rising. His *Crux* was strong because of practice and training, but he didn't know how long he could delay the *Auto-morphosis* into his *Animus*, his animal hunting form.

Once he turned into a panther, his vital hunger would force him to secure the viscera he needed. Hunting humans remained a capital crime in their laws, and he didn't want to unleash his beastly nature in this island paradise. It would ruin the peace.

The weather, which seemed beautiful earlier, now appeared like a sign that all things that could go wrong just did. His only consolation was that people would be less likely to come out in this storm. There would be fewer victims and potential witnesses to his crime.

The safety of the people on the island would depend on the protection that he would erect around himself. He hoped his text to his mentor got through and *sustenance* would be on its way within a day or so. He would try to hold off the *Automorphosis* for as long as he could.

If help failed to arrive in two days, he dared not think about the choices left to him. To kill a human, a capital crime punishable by death; consume his own liver, which would make him insane; or end his own life.

The result for him would be the same—death.

For now, it was time for his defensive plan. He had scoped the area the first day he arrived for a potential shelter just for an incident such as this. The old grain barn, made of stone and clay tucked at the back of the compound just behind the hotel, was the ideal place. And as was his training, he brought everything that he would need with him. His *Impedio*, some sedatives, and a muzzle. He would restrain and barricade himself there until *sustenance* arrived.

His pounding heart threatened to deafen him. He took deep breaths to calm himself down, to slow his heartbeat and tap into his *Crux* to determine how many hours he had left before he would lose complete control of his *Animus*.

Six, maybe eight hours before my Crux breaks down.

He needed to be away from Anza before then. He had enough time to prepare the barn, to protect the people from him. And hopefully, he would have some time to spare to reassure Anza.

She would be alone during his confinement. He didn't want her to think that he had abandoned her.

Veren had been gone since six a.m. It was past noon now, and he still wasn't back.

He wasn't in his room, nor was he in any of the public areas of the inn. No one had seen him, and they doubted he went anywhere outside since it had been pouring rain since dawn.

Where is he?

Anza couldn't shake the hunch he was in trouble. Something dark loomed, and it would affect them both.

The verandah, which she grew fond of because of the moments she had spent with Veren, was now restrictive. A single text message wiped away the serenity they had enjoyed just a few hours ago. She could not stay there, just waiting and worrying about him.

Despite their connection, she knew little about him. He could be a fugitive from the law or a psychopath. But even as she enumerated every possible dire and dangerous scenario about him, she couldn't disregard the fact that he had been nothing but caring to her.

She was a runaway, and he knew about it. He could have done anything to her, and no one would have found out. He could have taken advantage of her many times—at the Lighthouse, when she was sick, and even last night. There were plenty of times she was alone with him, and if he had wanted to do her harm, it would have been easy for him.

She was pacing in her room when a knock sounded. She rushed to open it, but to her disappointment, Mrs. Bassig greeted her.

"Good afternoon, Anza. I heard they cancelled your flight." Her cheerful voice grated on her nerves. Mrs. Bassig was carrying folded bedsheets, towels, and pillowcases.

"Good afternoon, Mrs. Bassig." She stepped aside to let her in. "Yes, Ma'am. I think they rescheduled it for tomorrow."

Mrs. Bassig handed her fresh bedclothes, and paused by the bed when she saw the backpack.

"All packed?" Mrs. Bassig said over her shoulder as she stripped the bed of its sheets with a quick, efficient motion. "You must be excited to go home to your family," she continued as she took one of the fresh sheets from her and redressed the bed.

"Yes, I am."

"I'm glad Veren was able to convince you to go home. While I would have loved for you to work with us, I was quite worried about you, as you are very young." Mrs. Bassig prattled on as she stripped the pillows' old cases and replaced them with fresh ones.

"And thank you for your generosity, Ma'am. I truly appreciate that you offered me the job." She would never forget how the older woman came to her rescue with no qualms.

"Did you call your father yet? He must be waiting for your homecoming," Mrs. Bassig mumbled as she stripped the second bed and peeled the cases from the pillows.

Anza shook her head. "Not yet, Ma'am. I need to charge my phone still. It might be flat." She found the tediousness of their exchange grating. She was worried about Veren and would rather go look for him.

"Oh, I'm sure Veren has informed your father already," Mrs. Bassig said as she fixed the new sheets on the bed. "He's an efficient emissary," she added as she tucked the ends of the sheets under the mattress.

Emissary?

"What do you mean, Mrs. Bassig?" Anza had taken a step closer to the older woman, unable to believe her words.

"I'm sure your father made the right decision in sending Veren ... I like that boy," Mrs. Bassig continued, unaware of the

157

upheaval she created. She was busy shaking a pillow into a fresh case. She fluffed it and dropped it on the bed.

Anza's heart, already beating fast because of her anxiety over Veren's unknown whereabouts, stopped and sank like a leaden weight inside of her stomach.

My father sent Veren after me? That can't be true.

She had to find Veren to talk to him, to hear the truth from him. Maybe Mrs. Bassig misunderstood, or Veren just said that to protect her. There were a thousand other reasons that could have prompted Veren to say that to Mrs. Bassig.

She rushed out of her room to search for him and left Mrs. Bassig without a word, driven by undefinable emotions. The horror that Veren might have played her echoed in her head as she rushed to his room, but he wasn't there. His backpack was also missing.

Did he leave me? Her heart pounded even harder at the thought.

She ran down to the lobby. Like earlier, no one had seen him. She felt crushed and bewildered, but told herself not to jump to conclusions until she had spoken to him.

Where did he go?

Short of running around in the rain, where else could she search? She had no choice but to go back to her room.

Just as she turned the corner of the stairway, she noticed movement in a small stone building at the end of the hotel compound, close to the herb garden. Someone slipped inside the structure. She didn't see who it was, but her gut told her it was Veren.

She sprinted downstairs and ran the distance from the back door to the stone building. The pouring rain drenched her, but she didn't care. The heavy wooden door was ajar. She pushed it in, just enough so she could squeeze through. It was dark, musty, and smelled of grain and damp stones. A barn.

Unable to see the interior, she cautiously paused by the entrance and waited for her vision to adjust. But she sensed a movement inside, which raised the hairs at the back of her neck.

The sound of a panting man echoed from inside. It was Veren. Then another sound came from the depths of the dark interior. It was something unknown to her. It sounded like the whimper of a wounded beast.

She took a step forward, but faltered when a harsh voice stopped her.

"Anza, no!" An agonised call came from the corner, behind sacks of grain piled high like a wall. "Stay there!" The guttural command wasn't enough to dissuade her.

Her eyes adjusted to the dark, and she could now see the heavy sacks that had partially barred the door. It looked like Veren had created a floor-to-ceiling barricade, to keep himself inside. Judging from the uneven height of the stack, it was unfinished, likely from a lack of material.

"Veren," she whispered.

"Anza, please ... leave me ..." Veren's harsh voice reverberated against the stone walls.

His plea went straight to her heart. It propelled her to climb atop the unfinished stack. Veren was curled on his side. His entire body shook—it looked like he was in horrible pain. He had a dog muzzle on, and he had shackled himself to the stone wall with chains attached to a thick leather vest strapped tight around his torso. That familiar contraption, an *Impedio*, one that she had seen in every *Viscerebus* household, explained everything to her.

Veren is a Viscerebus.

An Aswang like her entire family.

That one item confirmed everything Mrs. Bassig said to her

earlier. Anger bubbled up inside her, threatening to explode. In its wake, the pain of betrayal.

He was her keeper because her father sent him. He meant to take her home because it was his mission to do so. And he was to gain her trust, her friendship, to convince her to come home.

She stood there, rooted on the spot by the competing urge to lash out, and to leave him, never to see him again.

"Anza, please go ... you can't be here," he pleaded through pain that roughened up his voice.

The tortured tone broke through her fury. She realised he was protecting her from his *reflexive transformation* because she was the closest viscera source around. Her thoughts cleared like a cloud blown away by the wind.

If she ran to hide and left him to his fate, he might break away from his shackles. His wall of grain sacks was incomplete. Escape from this barn would be possible. If that happened, he would be in danger of attacking one of the staff in the inn. The humans would go after him in retaliation. They would kill him.

But even if he escaped them, an attack like this, in a place like this island, would make national news. The *Tribunal* would consider this a direct violation of the *Veil of Secrecy*. They would end his life, because he had just exposed the *Viscerebus*.

Veren would be in trouble no matter what.

By instinct, she knew what had to be done. All her life, she had prepared for and imagined doing this to her family members—to give out the only valuable thing she had to offer them: her viscera.

The clock had run out on Veren. There was no way for the *sustenance* to arrive on time.

She was his only chance.

She jumped down from the sack and rushed to Veren's side.

He recoiled, crawling away from her. He held out his hand to ward her off.

"Anza, no! Stay away ... Go to your room. Please, I can't—"

"Shut up, Veren! You need my help."

She started looking around for tools to use. She might need to go back to the kitchen and get a sharp enough knife, and the first aid kit.

"How much time do you have before you shape-shift?" She heard the urgency in her own voice.

"I don't know ... An hour or less," Veren replied, giving her a confused look.

"Okay, I need you to hold on. I'll go to the lobby and ask for their first aid kit. And a knife." She turned away from him. "Hopefully, a very sharp knife," she muttered.

Veren's hand shot out and captured hers, stopping her.

"I have those in there," he gasped out, pointing at his backpack. It was lying unnoticed behind her.

She reached for it and dug for the kit inside, conscious of the time constraints. She took out two soft bags marked with a big red cross. The smaller one contained two small bottles of pills. Sedatives and antibiotics. She zipped that one shut.

The bigger one was what she was looking for. Inside it, she found three hard plastic cases. The biggest contained a scalpel, some surgical clips, clamps, a pair of scissors, and various suture needles and surgical threads.

The middle-sized one was the heaviest. It held a bottle of antiseptic, a smaller bottle of alcohol, plastic-wrapped bandages, and cotton pads.

A longer but slimmer case carried two individually packed sterile syringes and needles, and two tiny glass vials.

"Anza, what are you planning to do?" Veren asked. His face reflected his dawning suspicion and was aghast.

"You're going to *absorb* me, Veren. It's the only way to save you."

The firmness of her tone hid her own misgivings. She didn't want him to doubt her intent, or to argue. If he fought her in this, she could lose her nerve.

"No ... Anza, you don't have to do this." Veren's weakened denial was hopeful, contradicting his words.

"Veren, don't argue. I've made up my mind. This is the best option. You'll end up killing a hapless human if we don't do this. And they'll murder you in return."

She had taken out the scalpel and bottle of antiseptic, then hiked her t-shirt up, exposing her abdomen. She realised she didn't know how to start.

"Veren, I need you to help me, too. You'll have to guide me on where to make the incision."

Veren's sharp intake of breath made her pause. He must have seen the determination in her eyes, saw her fear of what she needed to do, and her anticipation of pain.

"Okay," he said. "Let me do it."

He took off his muzzle and fumbled at the straps of the *Impedio*, but he stopped. He kept the *Impedio* on. After a moment's hesitation, he took out the bottle of alcohol from his kit and squirted it on his hands, rubbing them vigorously. Then he grabbed the bottle of antiseptic from her. With shaking hands, he ripped open a package of cotton pads, twisted the cap off the bottle, and moistened the pads with it.

"Lean back, Anza, and hold your shirt up."

She half reclined against a sack of grain. He wiped her upper abdomen, under her right rib cage with the antiseptic-moistened cotton pad. With efficient motion, he took a syringe, fitted a needle in it, and took one glass vial from his kit. He began siphoning the contents into the syringe.

"This is anaesthesia," he muttered through gritted teeth.

Thank Prometheus for that.

She nodded in acknowledgement. Her breathing became shallow.

"Are you sure, Anza?" he asked again, his expression pained.

She swallowed and nodded once more. "I am. Hurry, before you run out of time."

She was conscious of the possibility that he could transform at any moment. She wouldn't have the strength to stop him should the *Impedio* fail to keep him restrained.

The first puncture was quick, like an ant bite. He dispensed a quarter of the contents of the syringe. She felt the liquid spread through her muscles in tiny tentacles, radiating outward from the puncture point. Three more injections followed, then it was done.

She breathed out in relief. Sweat beaded her forehead.

"How long before the anaesthesia takes effect?"

"A few minutes... I'll make this quick. But I have another vial if we need to ..." He was unable to finish his sentence.

While they waited in the pregnant silence, Veren busied himself by preparing the suturing needle he would use later. He fished out a towel in a sealed bag from the bottom of his backpack. She marvelled at his level of preparation, despite her efforts to regulate her breathing to arrest her growing panic.

"How come you have all these medical tools with you?" she asked to distract herself and lessen the tension in the air.

"It's part of an *Iztari* medical kit. A standard issue." He couldn't meet her gaze. "Tell me when the area feels numb."

Finally, she felt the numbness in her upper stomach.

"Veren, it's time."

He poured antiseptic on his hands and rubbed them together. He then took the scalpel from her, squirted alcohol gel on it, and spread it all over the blade.

"Ready?" he asked. His thumb and forefinger pressed on the area where he would make the incision.

She swallowed and nodded. "Yes." She took a deep breath; braced herself for the cut and averted her face so as not to see the blood.

The sharp end of the blade cut deep into her flesh. She winced, not in pain, but at the strangeness of skin and muscles getting sliced, and the flow of warm blood that poured out of the cut and ran down her torso. Then she felt a sharp twinge of pain as the blade reached deeper and cut through the sheath that surrounded her liver. It made her gasp and jerk.

"Sorry," Veren mumbled, his voice as pained as hers. One hand held her down to minimise her movement.

Her hands clenched on the t-shirt she held up while her body trembled at the pain, her abdominal muscles locked with tension. Tears leaked out of her tightly squeezed eyelids.

It was unlike any pain she had ever experienced.

"Relax, Anza. Deep breaths ..."

Veren's calm voice alerted her to her shallow breathing. With extreme effort, she followed his direction. He widened the cut to expose a bigger portion of her organ. Thankfully, the cutting of her muscles didn't hurt, giving her reprieve.

However, when he cut through her liver, though it was quick, she screamed. The sound reverberated in the barn. The pain almost made her lose consciousness. Through her fading alertness, she heard Veren slurp the piece he had taken from her. She was vaguely aware of Veren pinching the wound close; of his warm tongue as he licked the wound to stem the blood flow.

Cold sweat covered her body, her efforts not to hyperventilate forgotten. Every puncture of the curved needle as he sewed her up made her appreciate the power of the anaesthesia. But at every moment, she expected the return of the pain.

Veren worked quickly. His movements were practised and quick.

After what seemed like an eternity, he cut the excess suturing thread from the wound. With a gentle touch, he wiped her torso clean with the towel, then poured antiseptic on the cut. The last thing she remembered was Veren pressing a square bandage on the wound.

Then everything faded.

Veren panicked when Anza's body slackened. His thumb touched the pulse on her neck. It was strong and fast, but it slowed down to its normal pace after a while. He breathed a sigh of relief. She was fortunately unconscious.

His awareness of their surroundings came back. It was still pouring rain outside; the howling wind would have masked Anza's scream. His strained muscles loosened somewhat. The effects of Anza's liver strengthened and energised him, fortifying his *Crux*.

Then the enormity of Anza's sacrifice dawned on him. Gratitude and something else he couldn't comprehend engulfed him. It was his undoing—his tears flowed.

His bloodied hand picked up hers, and he kissed it with reverence. Every emotion he had inside him, he poured into that kiss. This child-woman in his keeping became his keeper. He was supposed to save her, and yet she became his saviour.

She did not know it, and she probably never would, but she would always own a part of him that no other person in this world ever would.

He unshackled himself from his *Impedio*. There was no need for it now. Her liver gave him a week before he would need *sustenance* again. He got out and washed the bloodied towel in the rain. He returned inside the barn to make sure Anza was comfortable. While she slept, he put away his things in the backpack and started dismantling his sacks of grain barricade, returning it to its previous location—stacked at the back of the barn.

He kept a close eye on her wound. It had stopped bleeding. When the rain abated, he slung his backpack on over his shoulder and lifted Anza in his arms. He was thankful that they didn't encounter anyone along the way as he carried her to her room.

He realised this was the second time he would have to undress her. Her shirt and jeans were damp from earlier. Like before, he kept his eyes averted, but this time, he didn't dress her in a bathrobe. He covered her with the sheet. Her cut bled a little. The blood seeped into the bandage, staining it. It would be easier to dress her wound if she had no clothes on.

After replacing the bandage, he took the shirt to her bathroom and washed it. There were spots of blood on it. He hung her jeans and wet underclothes to dry. His mind was occupied with worry and prayers that her wound wouldn't get infected.

He was thinking of getting to his room to change out of his own damp jeans when his phone rang. It was Edrigu.

"Veren, I have been trying to call you, but you were out of range. I was informed that your flight was cancelled. How are you doing?" His questions came out in a barrage. Edrigu knew he was due for his *sustenance* today.

"I'm well, Sir," he replied. "The storm made it hard to get a signal." He didn't know how to tell Edrigu what Anza did for him.

"Can you still hold on for another day? I will try my best to fly in *victus* for you tonight. Although, I'm not sure if our team in Tuguegarao can brave the weather," Edrigu said, forewarning in his tone.

"There's no need for it, Sir," he began. "Anza offered ... her liver to me." He choked down the emotions that rose in him.

"What? Wow!" A low whistle followed his words. "How is she?" Edrigu asked after a momentary silence.

"She's resting," Veren said. He didn't want to voice out his concern about infections, for fear he might manifest it into a reality.

"Do you have antibiotics in your supplies?" Edrigu asked, his perception of the situation clear. His calm tone implied that everything that happened was commonplace.

"Yes." Edrigu's question had bolstered his confidence.

"Good. Give her two doses as soon as she wakes up. Now, you need to call Manuu to assure him you're taking Anza home in another two days," Edrigu said.

His mentor's brisk manner reminded him not to be emotional, to think like an *Iztari*. That sobered him up.

"Should I tell him ... what Anza did for me?"

"I think it is Anza's decision to make. Ask her when she awakens," Edrigu advised.

"Okay, Sir. Thank you," he said. The load on his shoulder lightened with the support of his mentor. "By the way, Sir, if I need a chopper, just in case, would you be able to arrange one?"

"Yes, just let me know if, and when, you need it. I'll have one on standby," Edrigu assured him.

After he ended the call with Edrigu, he took a deep breath and dialled Manuu Soledad's number. Their call was formal, his emotions held in check, no trace of the agitation that ruled him. He assured Anza's father that Anza agreed to go home and that he would arrange it in two days when the weather improves. As expected, Manuu was impatient and wanted to send a helicopter to pick them up, but he told him the weather could make the trip dangerous.

Manuu asked to speak to Anza, perhaps to reassure

himself. He got out of it by telling him Anza was still unaware of him being an *Iztari,* which was technically true. He pacified Manuu with two promises: that Anza would call him after she learned the truth about him, and that he would call Manuu by tomorrow afternoon to reconfirm they got a flight back to the mainland for the following day.

Anza stirred awake a few minutes later. He rushed to her side. She tried to get up, but the wound on her abdomen made her flinch and flop back on the bed.

"How are you feeling?" he asked. The pallor of her skin worried him.

Anza touched the bandage and realised she was naked underneath. Her cheeks flamed in embarrassment.

"Anza, on my honour, my eyes were closed. I kept you undressed because it's easier to change your bandage, should I need to," he said in haste.

His agitation calmed Anza as she looked back at him. Her abashed expression faded and transitioned to a serene, assessing one.

"Veren, I need an explanation." Her quiet words were loud in his ears.

He sighed and nodded. "Yes, you do. I'm an *Iztari,* and your father sent for me to find you ..."

"My father asked for you specifically?"

"No. The *Chief Iztari* appointed me because I was the closest to your age. Your father told us you know how the system works and you would expect *Iztaris* to come after you. Your father didn't want to force you to come home. He doesn't want you to run away again. They ordered me to work undercover."

"So, the friendship ... all to get me to trust you? To convince me to go home?" Anza's tone was clipped.

"No ..." He swallowed, took a deep breath, and grasped her

hand in his. He wanted to be completely honest with her. She deserved nothing less. He caught her gaze and held it. "In the beginning, the goal was to get your trust. The friendship came naturally." He hoped that his sincerity got through her defensive wall. The indecisiveness in her face hurt. He rubbed his chest to ease the pain of it—losing her regard might be the price he had to pay.

"Is that why you called yourself my keeper?" Her question came after a long silence. She sounded uncertain.

"No, Anza. That, like our friendship, was unplanned, unexpected. It just happened, and I wouldn't have it any other way."

Anza's eyes held his. In earnestness and without words, he pleaded with her to believe him. He felt tears prick behind his eyes, and he swallowed hard to push them back. Anza's gaze softened. She smiled and reached out to touch his cheek.

He closed his eyes at the relief; the gratitude at whichever god in the universe had gifted Anza with such a generous heart. He caught her hand and pressed a kiss at the centre of her palm. Her hand closed on that kiss and pressed it to her own heart.

To him, that small action was the most beautiful, most excruciating thing he had ever seen in his life.

9   THE HOMECOMING

Veren watched Anza sleep in silence. He had given her
antibiotics and pain medication from his kit; and
requested the front desk to get some ibuprofen from the doctor
nearby for her use in the succeeding days. He told Mrs. Bassig
that Anza was suffering from a bad toothache. It was an acceptable reason for her not to question why Anza would be in her
bedroom for most of the next two days.

The next morning, with the sheet wrapped around her, he
assisted her to walk around her room for a few minutes. The
surgery exhausted her, so Anza spent a lot of time sleeping. Her
wound was healing well. Her *Erdia* genes helped heal her cut
faster. Not as fast as someone like him, but it was still quicker
than a human's.

He spoon-fed her, even when she refused. He also made
her do breathing and coughing exercises every time she was
awake to ensure that she didn't develop pneumonia. By the
evening, Anza was begging him to allow her to take a shower.
He would hear none of it.

They compromised with a partial sponge bath.

Just before bedtime, he convinced Anza to call her father. He moved to the verandah while father and daughter conversed. He wanted Anza to have the time and privacy to express to her father how she felt about her life, and what she wanted to do.

The call wasn't long, and Anza was crying by the time it ended. Worried, Veren went back to the room to comfort her. A tremulous smile accompanied her tears.

"Did everything go well with your father?" His heart was full of hope for her.

"Yeah, I apologised. He accepted it. I told him we'll go home the day after tomorrow. He wanted to send a helicopter for us, but I convinced him not to—I told him the flight is confirmed," She said, her tone light. She looked relieved.

"Did you tell him about the *absorption?*" He wanted to be ready when he faced Manuu Soledad.

"No." She shook her head, her eyes intent on him. "That was my decision. It remains mine alone," she whispered.

"Okay." He wasn't altogether sure if he agreed with that decision, but as Edrigu said, this was her province since it was her liver. *Absorption* was always a personal decision. He realised he hadn't thanked her yet, even if he felt it in his soul.

"Veren, what happens after?" Anza asked, her eyes focused on the corners of the sheet she was twiddling with her fingers.

He understood what she was asking about, what she was asking for.

"I don't know, Anza. I have to go home, and I have military training to focus on." He had three more weeks of holiday before he was due. He was torn between spending it with her or using the time to fortify his emotional defences against her, which she had demolished with ease.

"Will you keep in touch?" Anza asked after a while. She

seemed to have accepted the fact their lives would diverge, if not the day after tomorrow, soon after.

"Yes. I will," he said, response automatic. "If that's what you want," he added, not knowing if she wanted this friendship to continue.

The slowly widening smile on her face soothed the ragged edges of his bruised heart. "Yes, I would like that. Very much, actually."

He knew what the promise would cost him, but there was no question about giving it to her. He would keep in touch for as long as she wanted him to. The power to dictate how much of him she wanted in her life would be in her hands. He wouldn't hinder the spreading of her wings, no matter how it might lead her away from him forever.

Hopefully, she would need him until she was ready for the kind of love that he could give her. And she would still be there when he became ready to love her the way she deserved to be loved.

Loving an *Erdia* like her would be a short-lived bliss for an *Aswang* like himself. Most of the males of his kind knew this. That was why most of them avoided it—why he should avoid it still.

It was a heavy price to pay for the surrender of one's heart for eternity.

The hour of their flight back to the mainland flew by despite Anza willing for time to slow down. Veren was solicitous, almost overly so. He refused to let her carry anything, not even her backpack. He hovered over her like a mother hen. She allowed him to, because she knew it was his way of thanking her.

Her wound was healing well. It still stung, but compared to the remembered pain of the surgery, it was negligible. Apart from the inner soreness behind her ribs, no doubt from her traumatised muscles and injured liver, there was nothing wrong with her.

They had left the wound free of the bandage after the first night to allow it to heal faster. Today, Veren placed a plaster over it so it wouldn't get chafed by her blouse during travel.

She thought about what she did and asked herself if she regretted it. Her response was an easy no. The reason she did it had a logical justification for it, but why she gave it to Veren was harder to answer. It just felt instinctive. No rhyme or reason to it.

They sat in silence, side by side. Her head rested against his bicep by force of habit. It was the most natural thing to do when she felt like dozing off. Her heart hummed with her head on him like this, surrounded by his familiar warmth and smell. As she inhaled, she recognised the elusive scent she had been trying to identify in Veren—the telltale musk of a *Viscerebus* male.

Her heart smiled, and something settled in her like a missing puzzle piece found.

After a few minutes, Veren lifted his arm, settled her head against his chest, and pulled her close. His action was spontaneous, and nothing new between them. What she didn't expect was Veren's larger hand clasping hers up as soon as they sat down. He linked their fingers together, palm resting in palm. His hand tightened on hers periodically during the flight, as if he was reassuring her and himself.

Two hours on, they both declined meals. She wasn't that hungry, and she didn't want to relinquish his hand. He didn't seem inclined either.

The jolt of the touchdown registered in her heart, like a

final curtain call. Her father would be at the airport to pick her up. Veren would wait for his connecting flight to Manila. And, they would part.

———

They kept to their seats until they were the last passengers in the aircraft. They had no check-in luggage, nothing to delay the parting. As they walked on, they slowed their steps as much as they could. Before they turned into the arrival area, Veren stopped her.

"Anza"—he dropped her hand as he dug his phone out from his backpack—"here's my number. Take it as we might not have time to exchange numbers later when we see your father."

She grabbed her phone from her bag and typed it into her phone. "Shall I give you mine?"

"Text or call me later and I'll save it." He wanted to keep to his internal vow to let her take the lead in their relationship.

She dialled his number, her eyes on him. The phone rang, confirming the number he gave her. That was a burner phone, with a burner number. Normally, he would discard it after a case, as was their training, never to use it again. This time, the phone would remain in his possession. It would be his lifeline, a part of him that only she would own.

She smiled at him, satisfied. Then, she took a step forward, but he stopped her with a hand on her elbow. There was one more thing he had to do, and it required going against his own interest.

"Anza ..." He inhaled then let out his breath. "Remember Diego?"

She nodded. "Yes. Why?"

"He might call you in Manila ..." he mumbled. "I just wanted to warn you." He couldn't look her in the eye. He had given Diego the chance to usurp his position as her keeper. He could only hope that Anza wouldn't take him up on it.

"Okay." Her response was dismissive.

She took the information like it was of no consequence to her. He didn't know how to process her reaction. Then Anza grabbed his hand and pulled him toward the arrival area, where he knew her father would be waiting.

Her welcoming entourage was a party of four: her father, stepmother, a male cousin, and an uncle. They all enveloped her in warm hugs, their circle complete and exclusive.

And Veren was outside of that circle. Out of place. He watched them admonish her gently in between kisses and hugs. These people clearly loved her. She would be safe and well-cared for.

"Mr. Albareda?" Manuu Soledad broke off from the group to shake his hand.

"Yes, Sir," he said. He kept his face impassive to quell the pain inside of him.

"Thank you for all the help. For getting her back to us. We owe you an enormous debt of gratitude that we cannot repay. If there is anything I can do for you, just say the word." Manuu Soledad's effusive gratitude rubbed him raw.

"Please, don't mention it, Sir. No gratitude is necessary." It was time to restart his life. "I have to go, Sir, as I have my Manila flight to catch." He shook Manuu's hand.

He turned towards the departure area, his back ramrod straight. As he walked away, he kept his eyes forward—he didn't want to look back and see Anza's face. He felt panicked at the idea of saying goodbye to her, and mournful for not being able to.

One regret was eating at him, he just realised.

He had wanted to kiss Anza, maybe since the first time he saw her. He never allowed the thought to surface, to even consider it. Her age, his age, their situation—all had stopped him.

At this moment, he would have given anything for that one brief kiss. But it seemed the kiss would have to wait for the right time, the right circumstances.

Just as he turned the corner towards the departure area, compulsion made him steal a last glance towards Anza. Her family still surrounded her, but through the gaps between the multiple arms wrapped around her, their eyes connected in the distance. There was a question in her gaze and a promise in his.

For his life, she willingly gave him a piece of her liver, an organ that she could regenerate. For her sacrifice, he gave her his heart.

Unfortunately for him, he couldn't regrow a heart.

10 THE RETURNING HEART

Six years later.

Veren was on the third day of his first-ever holiday since he became an *Iztari*. They had promoted him: a reward for a hard two years of war to subdue a rebellion among their kind. It was an arduous battle. He almost died during two encounters, but he fought on. The vow he made to himself made him want to live.

The war ended, but the danger of another one was never far from their minds. It caught the *Supreme Viscerebus Tribunal* unaware and, as a result, it endangered the lives of every one of their kind from the humans that outnumbered them.

His mentor, Edrigu Orzabal, had formed a small band of *Iztaris*, designed to work in complete secrecy to spy, and to preempt any other potential uprising.

Before they started their official operation, they were all given a chance to rest, recuperate, and fulfil any unfinished business they had left behind. Veren intended to do all of that. If there was something the previous war had taught him, it was that time was fleeting, and he shouldn't let it bleed away without doing everything in his power to achieve the personal happiness that he craved.

He selected this location for his first Transit, not for the scenery or the lifestyle. His reason to be here was more compelling. He was on a search and recovery mission—a personal one.

And according to confidential records, Anza had moved here.

After the war, he needed to find her. He realised that he had searched for her every day in the most elemental of levels. His work may have occupied his waking hours, but she was never far from his thoughts. She was with him during the lull of each day, the minutes just before he fell asleep, and most often, she appeared in his dreams.

In the early months of their separation, her messages were friendly, sweet, and innocent. She filled it with accounts of her days, which made his heart ache with longing, and the worst parts were when she reminisced about their days in Basco. That broke his heart every time.

As he had promised himself, he adopted the same tone as her messages, but with fewer details. He didn't want to clip her wings as she learned how to fly, nor did he want to anchor her to the ground when she needed to soar.

The frequency of their exchange dwindled as the contents of her messages changed. It became filled with mentions of other people in her life, new routines and activities. She stopped communicating with him after one year. That is, after Anza's family left for their Transit.

He wondered if she had changed, if she was still into photography, music, and poetry. If she still thought about their days in Basco.

Now, six years after the fact, he was hot on her trail. One of Edrigu's gifts to him was access to the Soledad family's *Transit* file. He knew she was here in Madrid, but not her exact address. He would have to do some digging from the local *Tribunal*. One lead was the Biblioteca Nacional. He had a gut feeling that would lead him to Anza.

Intuition led him to her that first time. Hopefully, it would guide him to her this time.

Anza closed the book *The Matriarchy—Five Hundred Years of Progressive Viscerebus Existence in the 21st Century*. For the past five years, she read as much as she could about the lives of the *Viscerebus* to make up for the years she ignored that part of her heritage.

She grew up with her *Aswang* kin, bound herself to the *Veil* that ruled them, yet she had never attempted to get to know them deeper. That was a mistake. She limited herself to knowing her immediate family, but not into understanding them at a core level. She knew their laws, but not why the laws became necessary.

Her thoughts, as usual, dealt with Veren, her Keeper, whenever she touched upon the subject. She wondered what he was doing at the moment. They had lost touch five years ago when her old phone fell into the sea when they boarded the cruise ship to Europe. It was a holiday before they settled in New Zealand for their *Transit*.

She was frantic about it when it happened, but she realised maybe it was meant to be. His previous replies to her messages had become shorter and impersonal. The last one was a single word—"Okay," which took him two days to send. Perhaps he got busy with work as an *Iztari*. It could be that he moved on with his life. One that did not include her.

She then focused her attention on enjoying the freedom she won from her parents. It was hard fought, but it was well worth it. She now lived the life of a human. Her father had given her a reasonable amount of autonomy, with just one caveat—none of her family members would be photographed, mentioned, or recorded in any of her correspondence and social media, except in the most superficial of ways. Also, she needed to spend at least three months a year in Auckland with them.

When they *Transited*, she had a choice to keep in contact with her friends by phone, but not with her social media. She kept that account active for two years, hoping that Veren might contact her there, but at his continued silence, she relented and deactivated it.

Two years after they settled in New Zealand, she moved to Madrid to study. And here she had stayed since. She'd made close friends here, a circle of five girls including Elyse and Rizzi. They had maintained their friendship since high school. Elyse and Rizzi elected to study in Madrid and she found the idea attractive. Summer had been crossing over from Paris twice a year.

She spent her days on her creative endeavours—writing and composing songs for some upcoming singers in the country. Her life became more balanced, more satisfying. Richer and nuanced. However, the sense of contentment that she was trying to recapture remained elusive.

Veren resurfaced in her consciousness and had taken up much of her thoughts in the past two years, because of the political crisis that assailed the *Viscerebuskind*. The conflict had escalated to a degree that it almost became a full-blown global war. Her concern for Veren's welfare became constant.

Reading the *Tribunal Journal* as soon as it got released became a priority. She scouted for news about the *Iztaris*, about him.

She put the book back on the shelf. It was time to meet her friends near Puerta de Alcala. A glance at the overhead clock in the library told her she was running late. She would have to walk as fast as she could to arrive on time. Diego, a long-time friend, had flown in from Manila and she didn't want to make him wait.

All her friends rooted for Diego. They thought it very romantic that he always came to Madrid at this time of the year for his annual holiday. Diego hadn't been secretive about his desire to be more than friends with her since the very beginning, but she felt she was too young for a relationship back then. Also, she had to admit that her memories of Veren hindered her inclination towards other boys her age. They all seemed too juvenile, too shallow, too insubstantial.

Diego was selfless enough to accompany her through her journey of personal growth and learning about the world and its human inhabitants. He had been a good and constant friend over the years, and he was one of the few humans she maintained contact with after the *Transit*.

Her close relationship with her cousin Xandrei balanced her view of the two kinds of people in her life, and she realised she was quite lucky. She lived between two worlds, allowed to cross either at will. Most of her *Vis* did not have that freedom, and the humans didn't even know of the other. Diego remained ignorant of her nature and her family, so trust between them never deepened.

As she walked down the stairs of the library, she thought that if she was going to have a boyfriend now, she could do no better than Diego. Attractive, smart, kind and steadfast. She trusted him, and she knew Diego loved her.

Her mind was preoccupied with the thoughts of the past,

present, and wishes for her future as she rushed towards her destination.

Anza traversed the streets by instinct while she sent a text message to her friends to inform them she would be ten or fifteen minutes late. She was familiar with the streets of Madrid, and had walked them almost every day since she moved here. She slid her phone back into her bag and turned into the corner of an alley that would cut her travel time in half.

As Veren turned the street corner, a woman crashed into him, almost bouncing off of him. By instinct, his hand shot out to steady her. That simple touch electrified him. His entire being knew before the woman looked up.

Anza.

Her gasp of recognition echoed his sharp intake of breath. His brain reeled, dizzying him as his world staggered to a complete stop. He didn't know how long he stood there gazing at her. She looked equally stunned and thunderstruck. Her eyes locked onto his.

All his senses focused on her and her sweet face. Familiar, yet new. The baby soft cheeks were less so, her eyes were still as wide, and her lips had the same plump pout. All those years apart, the tame, friendly messages in the early months, and the complete silence in the last five years, came rushing back to him.

The pressure in his heart bubbled over, and a burst of instinct overpowered him. He pulled her flush into his arms, her hands flattened between them, palms rested over his pounding heart. His mind had only one overwhelming thought: to kiss Anza. *Finally.*

His iron control was stretched taut. His sense of honour

compelled him to ask for permission from her. But the words wouldn't come. His lips were almost touching hers, his shuddering breath an entreaty as he waited in pained silence for her.

Anza's own breath trembled before she breached the hairline gap between their lips. Her agreement was like an explosion to his senses. That was enough.

His lips fastened onto hers like a man dying of thirst. It was a fierce, demanding, pleading kiss. Anza's indrawn breath was lost in his mouth, her head cradled in his hand as he anchored her for his kiss, savouring the texture of her mouth.

Her scent enveloped him; the softness of her clouded his vision. She still smelled the same, still felt the same. Except that she was a woman now. Ready for the love he wanted to give her. And his heart quickened as she kissed him back with equal intensity. The same longing flavoured her kisses. The same feeling of homecoming suffused them both.

All the emotions he had bottled up inside, so he could function during those years of radio silence, all the feelings he refused to shine a light on as a matter of self-preservation, converged into this one single moment.

He ripped his mouth off from her when the pressure on his chest threatened to burst. He leaned into her; their foreheads touched. His arms wrapped like tight bands around her. His very being wanted to absorb her into himself, never to part with Anza again. He kept his eyes closed. To look into hers would unman him.

"Anza," he breathed out into her mouth. His throat refused to move for the words he wanted to say to her. He swallowed to loosen it.

"What took you so long?" She rested her cheek on his chest.

"Life goals ... You needed to grow up, and I needed to be ready for us."

"And are you ready now?" Her voice came soft as a whisper.

"Yes ... No more wasting time."

Her sigh of contentment went straight to his soul.

And everything in his world righted itself. In her presence, he felt his heart grow back.

THE END

Dear reader,

We hope you enjoyed reading *The Keeper* Please take a moment to leave a review, even if it's a short one. Your opinion is important to us.

Discover more books by Oz Mari G. at https://www.nextchapter.pub/authors/oz-mari-g

Want to know when one of our books is free or discounted? Join the newsletter at http://eepurl.com/bqqB3H

Best regards,

Oz Mari G. and the Next Chapter Team

WORLD OF THE VISCEREBUS GLOSSARY

THESE ARE THE VISCEREBUS TERMS MENTIONED IN THE NOVEL.

Absorption—or ***Zurugatzen***—the voluntary practice of offering one's own viscera upon death to select Viscerebus loved ones. This is practiced by Viscerebus, Veil-bound Erdias, and in rare cases, Veil-bound humans. The offered organs are consumed or 'absorbed' by the Viscerebus recipient. This is an act of love and faith that once absorbed, the donor, or *Rugat*, becomes part of the recipient, or the *Zurugat*, forever. The ritual is usually between parent and child, siblings, life partners and lovers. (*See Zurugatzen – The World of Viscerebus Almanac*).

Animus (Heart or Instinct Animal) or Spirit Animal — the true animal form of a Viscerebus. All Viscerebus have one, although not all would discover theirs. An *Auto-morphosis*, or *reflexive transformation*, usually reveals to a Viscerebus their Animus. Some Viscerebus transform into one animal all their lives and discover that their Animus was a different form.

In some Viscerebus families, it was part of their tradition to deny sustenance to the child of twelve to force an Auto-morphosis. This is usually done under the supervision of the adults. The practice lost favour over the centuries because it often resulted in injury to the child and usually the said child would elect to transform into the animal form they habitually turn into, thus defeating the object of discovering their Animus.

Now, the term is used erroneously by modern Viscerebus to refer to their animal form, whether it is their true Spirit Animal or just their hunting form. (*See Auto-morphosis. See Spirit Animal, Reflexive Transformation – The World of the Viscerebus Almanac*).

Apex – A super shapeshifter. A very rare Viscerebus that can transform into a winged animal, either chiropteran (bats) or avian (birds) form. They can transform fully, or partially. Other special Apex skills that previous ones have manifested are echolocation, sound blasting, and magnetic field manipulation.

Natural facial alteration for disguise is a skill Apex Kazu Nakahara discovered. For an Apex that becomes skilled in turning on their brain's theta waves, they can read other people's brain waves and influence them.

It is said that the full skill set of an Apex has not been fully revealed yet because new skills keep getting discovered by each successive Apex. (*See Shape-shifting – The World of the Viscerebus Almanac, Dawn of the Dual Apex*)

Aquila—the other name for the giant eagle named Aetos Kaukasios, one of the two primary mythical gods to the Viscerebus. The other is Prometheus. The Viscerebuskind attribute the beginning of their race to the two gods. According to the legend, Zeus sent Aetos to devour the liver of Prometheus every night as his eternal punishment for giving fire to humans and for tricking Zeus to choose a less valuable sacrificial offering from humans. The Viscerebus' need to eat viscera is attributed to the saliva of Aetos believed to have contaminated the liver of Prometheus, which was used by the latter to create the Viscerebus.

Aetos was the offspring of two other Titans, Typhon and Echidna, the father and mother of mythical monsters in Greek Mythology. (*See Prometheus. See Origin – World of the Viscerebus Almanac*).

Aswangs – The Filipino term for Viscerebus. Of all the countries in the world, the existence of Viscerebus is the most entrenched in the Philippine culture for two reasons:

First, the Filipinos launched the most aggressive campaign against the Viscerebus. Their Venandis were the most experienced. The Venandi practice, which started as a family endeavour, became traditionally and habitually passed on to the next generation. There are still active—albeit a lesser number of—Venandis operating in the country.

The superstitious nature of the Filipinos allows them to believe that Aswangs still exist, albeit in exaggerated and erroneous form. Many books have been written, and movies made, featuring Aswangs as evil creatures, usually depicted as the minions of the devil.

Like every culture, the existence of the Viscerebus has been relegated into myth and lore, and the term Aswang is used as a blanket term for almost every man-eating and blood sucking ghoul in the country.

Second, the local tribes in the country were also the first to accept the Viscerebus into their midst and established a collaborative and symbiotic relationship. Native Viscerebus in the Philippines were the only ones sanctioned by the Tribunal to work openly with the human tribal members. Their Veilbinding applies only to humans that were not part of the tribe. (*See Venandi – World of the Viscerebus Almanac*).

Auto-morphosis – also known as *Reflexive Transformation* is the involuntary shape-shifting into the animal spirit of a Viscerebus. The vital instinct to hunt and secure *Victus* or *sustenance* triggers this transformation. It triggers the vital instinct when a Viscerebus fails to consume human viscera for over three days.

It is possible to induce an Auto-morphosis through practice and meditation. Some Viscerebus do this to discover their *Animus*. (*See Animus, Crux, Reflexive Transformation, See Shape-shifting – World of the Viscerebus Almanac*)

Brevis Amorem—or short love. A label used by the Vis community for a temporary romantic relationship or affair between a Viscerebus male and a human female. The chief characteristic is the initial intention of the male to conduct a short-term relationship with a female from the outset, regardless if the female is aware of or in agreement with it.

Most male Viscerebus use the Veil of Secrecy law to justify having multiple brevis amorems. It was normal and acceptable. The community called Viscerebus males who practise this as a

Hedonis. It had the same connotation as being a player, or a playboy in the human world.

In the most recent history, female Viscerebus embraced the practice as well, and claimed equal rights to conduct brief affairs with males, whether Vis or human. The fundamental distinction was their refusal to have kids with the males. It started as a way of rebelling against the societal expectations for females to give birth to a new generation of Viscerebus.

To call a female *Hedonis*, or a **Hedonna,** was derogatory. Most female Viscerebus resented the label. However, the stigma falls away the moment a female Vis gives birth. The Viscerebus society considers them to have done their duty in the propagation of their kind. A woman could return to Brevis Amorem practice and never again be looked down upon.

Recent times, however, revived the title, and the Viscerebus women wear it proudly. (*See Hedonna, Hedonis – The World of the Viscerebus Almanac*)

Crux—the subconscious inner control of a Viscerebus to stop or start shapeshifting into their animal form. A Viscerebus could call forth their Crux into consciousness to prevent an *Auto-morphosis* or *reflexive transformation*. A Viscerebus can strengthen their Crux through meditation and constant practice.

It is common training for *Iztaris* and some individuals to embark on regular vital fasting to flex and strengthen their Crux.

The Crux is similar to human willpower. (*See Auto-morphosis, Reflexive Transformation, See Vital Fasting – The World of the Viscerebus Almanac*)

Erdia—an Erdia is a half-blood, born from a Male Viscerebus and a Female human. Erdias are very human in their nature except they would be slightly stronger, faster and live longer than their human counterpart. They may inherit some enhancement on their senses. They don't inherit the shape-shifting and need for human viscera.

Most Erdias who use their enhanced strength and speed become athletes. Erdias who inherit a superior sense of taste and scent usually become renowned chefs, perfume makers and other professionals that maximise their abilities.

The knowledge of the Erdias about the Viscerebuskind would depend on whether the Viscerebus father tells his offspring. If the Erdia was told, they would be bound to the Veil of Secrecy just like their Viscerebus parent, and they become part of the Viscerebus world.

A significant number of Erdias are unaware of the Viscerebus world because the Viscerebus father abandons them from infancy. These Erdias, being non-Veil-bound, are treated as human. They live normal human lives, unaware of the existence of the Viscerebus. (*See Eremite, Mejordia – World of the Viscerebus Almanac*).

Gentem — (nation in Latin)–the current country of residence, or the immediate, previous country of residence of a *Transitting* Viscerebus. A Viscerebus can have between six to ten Gentems in their lifetime. This is not to be confused with **Patriam**, which is the country of birth of a Viscerebus. (*See Patriam – World of the Viscerebus Almanac.*)

Impedio – a leather vest and chain contraption meant to restrain a Viscerebus from attacking humans during Auto-morphosis, or reflexive transformation. It is strapped tightly to the body of the Vis; the chains are attached to a firm foundation, like a wall or a tree. And when appropriate, a muzzle is part of the set. Every Vis is required to own one and carry it with them when they travel to remote places, especially if they travel for over three days.

The modern Impedio has a Tracking Device that is automatically triggered when the Distress Transmitter is turned on. The Distress Transmitter can be activated manually and automatically by the change of the heartbeat in a Vis during complete transformation.

The transmitter signals the nearest Iztari office that someone needs human viscera. The Iztaris are then deployed to rescue the unfortunate being.

It is illegal to activate a Distress Transmitter as a joke or a prank. The punishment comprises a huge fine, and a demerit point on their record. (*See Auto-Morphosis, Reflexive transformation, See Demerit System – The World of the Viscerebus Almanac*)

Iztari—the law enforcement of the Supreme Viscerebus Tribunal. They are embedded in the human armed forces, police and security community as a way of hiding in plain sight, acquiring military training and gaining knowledge on the human military and police system.

The Iztaris' main mandate is to implement strict adherence to the Veil of Secrecy. They are deployed to either a) hunt

Harravirs or Harravis, b) implement the Veil procedures, c) defend humans or other Viscerebus from Harravirs and Harravises, d) Find other Viscerebus communities.

The Iztari system is unique, as there are no ranks among the Iztaris. However, there is a Team Head appointed when a team is deployed. The only figure of authority is the Chief Iztari. The Iztari office employs both Viscerebus and Erdias with the right skills. Erdias are office bound and do analyst and research tasks rather than fieldwork.

Only the Viscerebus may go on field because of the inherent danger of dealing with a vicious Harravir and Harravis. Iztaris are well-trained and well-equipped for combat. The Iztari office uses the latest technologies that the human and the Viscerebuskind can offer. Ten per cent of the Viscerebi population are Iztaris. (*See SVT – World of the Viscerebus Almanac*).

Prometheus—A Greek Titan and the god of creative fire and the creator of men. He was the son of Titan Iapetus and the Oceanids, Clymene. His siblings are Atlas, Epimetheus, Menoetius. He is known for his intelligence, as the author of human arts and sciences, and a champion of humankind. His name meant "Forethought".

According to the Viscerebus legends, while he created humans out of clay, Prometheus made the first Viscerebus couple from his own liver, the soil and rocks of the Caucasus mountain where he was bound and tortured.

With his DNA, the Viscerebus inherited godlike traits of super strength, speed, senses, healing abilities and long life. Prometheus also imbued them with the ability to shape-shift so they can hide themselves from Zeus.

It was said that he created them out of his need for companions to distract himself from the pain of having his liver eaten every day by Aetos, and the loneliness during the regrowing of the organ every night.

During the day, the first Viscerebus were in their animal form, a feline and a canine, but they transform into their human form at night to keep Prometheus company. This is also why cats and dogs were regarded as the closest companions to humans. (*See Origin – World of the Viscerebus Almanac*)

Reflexive Transformation – also referred to as *Auto-morphosis*, the involuntary transformation or shape-shifting into the animal spirit of a Viscerebus. The vital instinct to hunt and secure sustenance triggers this transformation. This instinct, in turn, is triggered when a Viscerebus fails to consume sustenance, weakening the Crux, the subconscious and internal control of a Viscerebus to retain their human form. Once weakened, a Viscerebus' human form becomes unstable. Once sustenance is consumed, Crux control is regained, and the Viscerebus can shift back to their human form with ease.

It is possible to induce a Reflexive Transformation through practice and meditation. (*See Auto-morphosis, Impedio*)

Shape-shifting – one of the primary traits of a Viscerebus. This is closely related to their need to consume human viscera. The viscera stabilises the human form of a Vis. The prolonged absence of a victus, usually three days, triggers the vital hunger and kicks in vital instinct to hunt. Once vital instinct is triggered, the Vis transforms reflexively into their Animus. A Vis has a conscious control of their shape-shifting at most times, through their Crux. (*See Auto-morphosis, Reflexive Transformation. See All about the Vis – World of the Viscerebus Almanac.*)

Supreme Viscerebus Tribunal – or the SVT. This is the primary ruling body of the Viscerebus. It is composed of previous and current Matriarch and Patriarchs from different Gentems all over the world. SVT functions as both the main legislative and judicial body of the Viscerebi. The execution of the laws, however, is the responsibility of each Gentem's Tribunal. Members of the body meet bi-annual, where laws proposed by members are discussed and voted on. The main mandate of the Tribunal is to oversee the compliance of every Gentem in the upholding of the Veil of Secrecy. The SVT is the ultimate rule of law for the Viscerebi. (*See Veil of Secrecy. See 5000BCE Constitution, Implementing Rules and Regulations – World of the Viscerebus Almanac*).

Sustenance– or *Victus.* The blanket term used by Viscerebus to refer to human viscera that they take regularly. This is crucial to stabilising the human form of a Viscerebus. This is the term used by modern Viscerebus, as the term does not invite unnecessary questions and explanations. (*See Crux, Auto-morphosis, Reflexive Transformation. See Victus, Vital hunger – World of the Viscerebus Almanac*).

Transit—The program of relocating a Viscerebus and his/her family to maintain the Veil of Secrecy. A Viscerebus can be under a Life Transit, a mandatory, scheduled relocation every thirty years; or a Forcible Transit, unscheduled relocation because of the Viscerebus' violation of the Veil. A Forcible Transit is equivalent to an exile in human government.

A Transitting Viscerebus is required to cut contact with any of their *non-Veil-bound* human or Erdia friends, relatives and connections. But they can keep contact with other Viscerebus and Veil-bound Erdia friends, relatives and connections.

A Transitting Viscerebus may keep his or her old name and profession, or may take on a new one. The new Transit location has to be in a different country or continent. A Transitting Viscerebus can return to their *Patriam* or previous *Gentem* after 100 years to ensure that any human they had a relationship with before are already dead. Visits to the Patriam and previous Gentems are permitted on brief holidays and only once every ten years. Veil of Secrecy restrictions apply. (*See Veil of Secrecy. Gentem, See Patriam, Transit Program – World of the Viscerebus Almanac*)

Veil of Secrecy—the inviolable law of the Tribunal to keep the existence of Viscerebus a secret from non-Viscerebus. The Law made exceptions to a) Human spouse; b) Human kids. However, the exceptions apply only if the above people prove themselves loyal to the Viscerebuskind and to the Veil.

The strict adherence to the Veil guides every interaction of a Viscerebus with humans and non-Veil-bound Erdias. The violation or breaking of the Veil would entail severe punishment that could cause the death of the human or the non-Veil-bound Erdia, and the violator is expected to execute the punishment. (*See SVT, or Supreme Viscerebus Tribunal. See 5000BCE Constitution – World of the Viscerebus Almanac*).

Victus – colloquially called as *Sustenance*. This is the blanket term for human viscera, heart, liver and kidney, that a Viscerebus must consume regularly to keep their Vital Hunger at bay and prevent involuntary transformation to their animal form.

This term had become less popular than its colloquial counterpart as humans who overheard ask question what it means. The Tribunal encourages the use of the term *Sustenance* in a public setting to avoid the questions. (*See Sustenance, Crux, Auto-morphosis, Reflexive Transformation, Vital Hunger*)

Viscerebus/Viscerebi (pl.)—or Viscera-eaters, colloquially known as **Vis**. They are a different species of human. They live two to three times longer than a human, are stronger, faster, and have quick healing abilities.

Physically, they look exactly like humans, but they can shape-shift into a land-based predator. The Viscerebus need to eat human viscera to stabilise their human form. To normal humans, they are monstrous man-eaters.

Viscerebi are known by many names in many cultures. And the descriptions vary because of the dilution of the truth engineered by the Tribunal to bury the existence of the Viscerebus under myth and lore. The common thread among these lores is the shape-shifting and the viscera-eating.

Most modern human societies have completely ignored the lores, but the belief persists in some pockets of rural communities all over the world. This is especially true in Asian countries, particularly the Philippines, where stories about Aswangs, the local name for Viscerebus, are still told to this day. (*See Aswang*)

Vital Hunger—the term used to refer to the need to consume *Victus,* or *sustenance.* The sensation is similar to physical hunger, but it pertains to the need of a Viscerebus to secure sustenance to keep their Crux strong and prevent an Auto-morphosis. This manifests if the Vis has neglected to consume sustenance for at least three days. This triggers the *vital instinct* to hunt, which, in turn, triggers the Auto-morphosis, or reflexive transformation.

The symptoms are usually a loss of energy and physical weakening of the Viscerebus. Some Vis develop physical hunger-like symptoms, like shaking and trembling. Vital hunger itself is not painful, but the accompanying pain comes from the battle between the body's Crux and the vital instinct. (*See Auto-morphosis, Crux, Reflexive Transformation, Vital Instinct*)

Vital Instinct—the basic survival instinct of a Viscerebus to consume *Victus,* or human liver, heart or kidney. While this could be interchangeable to the term *Vital Hunger,* this refers to the instinct to hunt rather than the hunger to consume. This surfaces when a Viscerebus fails to partake of human viscera for over three days. At this point, there is a battle between the Vital Instinct and the Crux of the individual.

The stronger the Crux, the longer the Viscerebus can control the transformation. However, inevitably, the Vital Instinct wins, thus forcing an Auto-morphosis, or the reflexive transformation into the Viscerebus' Animus. Once the Vital hunger is quenched, it restores the Crux control of the Viscerebus. (*See Crux, Auto-morphosis, Reflexive Transformation, Vital Hunger*).

Vondenad (Vondenada, f, Vondenado, m) – from the Dutch word "vondeling". The Viscerebus term for "foundling." This refers to the Veil-bound offsprings of any male or female Viscerebus and Erdias that were abandoned by their parents. Although the term used is not the same as an orphan (*Aulila*) or a runaway (*Reneweg*), they are all taken into custody and become a ward of the Supreme Tribunal.

Unlike in human practices, most Vondenados and Vondenadas are immediately taken into the custody of the Tribunal. And they are assigned a foster family, or a *Thetadom* within thirty days. It is illegal to treat a Vondenado/Vondenada as an outsider while they are within the care of a foster family.

Foster parents (*Theta and Thetos*) are expected to care for their ward like their own child and teach them the ways of life and the rules of the Tribunal. They function like a mentor and a parent combine. A Viscerebus or Erdia family could only take on a maximum of one Vondenado or Vondenada every five years. Exceptions are made for siblings. They are usually placed together in one home.

Most foster parents end up adopting the child in their care. Adoption would only be approved when the child reaches the age of eighteen. However, the choice is left to the child whether they would like to be adopted or remain to be a protégé. More than half the Vondenado/Vondenadas opt for the latter because they do not feel like they belong, or they prefer the independence. (*See Aulila, Reneweg, Thetadom, Thetas and Thetos – The World of the Viscerebus Almanac*)

Note: All novels in the World of the Viscerebus series contain a glossary of terms used in the respective books. The full glossary of terms and other information can be found in the WORLD OF THE VISCEREBUS ALMANAC.

AFTERWORD

Dear Reader,

I have built the World of the Viscerebus as richly as I could with stories that are exciting, entertaining and stimulating to the mind. Viscerebus is my global word for the viscera-eaters that are prevalent in various cultures, especially in Southeast Asia. They are known as Aswang in my country.

In this fantasy world, there is the main storyline, a trilogy: Rise of the Viscerebus, First Chronicle; Dawn of the Dual Apex, Second Chronicle, and InEquilibrium, Third Chronicle.

Then there are the companion novels namely Beasts of Prey, The Keeper, and two others that are still works in-progress.

To improve on this fantasy world further, your feedback is valuable to me. If you can please leave a review of my book on Amazon or through the email listed below, I would appreciate it very much.

Or, if you wish to be part of the select early readers of my works, please let me know via email at marigr8@yahoo.com. And follow me at Twitter @GraceGranlund, Instagram @Gogranlund, or Facebook Oz Mari Granlund

Thank you.

Oz Mari G.

The Keeper
ISBN: 978-4-86750-671-4

Published by
Next Chapter
1-60-20 Minami-Otsuka
170-0005 Toshima-Ku, Tokyo
+818035793528

7th June 2021

Lightning Source UK Ltd.
Milton Keynes UK
UKHW041615240621
386092UK00001B/108